BLACK HAND

MAYA DANIELS

BOOKS

By Maya Daniels

Infernal Regions for the Unprepared

Black Hand

Lower World

Everlasting Fire

Place of Torment

Vinci Books

vinci-books.com

Published by Vinci Books Ltd in 2025

1

Chapter One

I was unprepared.

I wasn't ready for the curve ball life was about to throw at me.

Nor did I anticipate what the fates had in store for the near future.

The tiny pinpricks of light reflected through the window of the plane, the city below the metal bird stretching over the hills as far as I could see. I mushed my face closer to get a better look, but the glass fogged from my breath. My stomach dropped when we lost altitude, the winds lashing at the plane making the last fifty minutes of the flight turbulent and unsettling. If it went down, it'd solve a lot of my problems. Although …

I was unprepared for that, as well.

I wanted to live.

My heart skipped a beat when the light blinked on above my head for the seatbelt, the loud chime echoing through my head like a gong going off. The plane was made for humans, not creatures like me with super-sensitive hearing. Being an *Atua* was seen as fiction in this world. They liked to call us vampires, but little did they know we were very much real, we lived among them, we manipulated their lives for our gain, and we had no remorse at all. Well, most of my kind didn't. I, on the other hand, was cursed ... or something. I cared a little too much.

I should've expected my reaction to get attention, but I did not. It would've saved me a lot of hassle if I didn't flinch like a rookie. Too late I noticed the flight attendant beelining my way with a look of determination on her face. Her hands were swinging by her body in fast, sharp jerks as her legs scrunched her skirt above her knees from her long strides. The woman was on a mission and there was no mistaking that.

You'd think she was about to fight a crocodile to save my life.

"You doing okay there, doll?" Her brown gaze locked on my face, the expression there telling me I'd better not lie to her, and her hairstyle with not a single hair out of line said, "Don't mess with me.".

"I'm good, thank you." Offering a small smile that was more a press of my lips than anything else, I stared at her chin. A bad habit I'd developed through the years so I could keep my eyes hidden. They gave away the fire scorching my insides from the anger I'd internalized for centuries. To humans they were just freaky, I guessed.

"She gets nervous when flying," Veronica chirped from next to me, shifting in her seat and flipping her blonde ponytail over her shoulder with a delicate hand. "She'll be fine as soon as we land."

"We are almost there." The Flight attendant gave me a once over as if checking for tells that I wasn't being truthful.

"Keep your seats up and put your seatbelts on. Around this time of the year, the winds don't make it easy for those that get jittery on a flight."

"Will do," we both piped in with tight smiles aimed at the attendant, and I turned to look out the window again because I was done talking. I heard her footsteps slowly walking away after about a minute, and she'd probably stared at the back of my head that whole time.

"Stay alert. You're slipping," Veronica murmured under her breath, her words too low for anyone but me to hear her. "Snap out of it before we have the same situation we had three years ago."

"Right." Ignoring her jab about my trip to the cages—where I spent an entire year in darkness with barely any blood to keep me alive—I kept my eyes glued to the glass, seeing nothing, though her words did send a ping straight through my gut. My fingers trailed over the inside of my left forearm, the phantom pain reminding me of the ripped flesh that used to be there regardless of the smooth skin covering it now. The cruel voices laughing and gloating at my pain while they teared my flesh were trying to drown me, but I clenched my jaw and pushed them away. I would not dwell on that now.

Not ever.

Immortality was seen as a blessing by humans, their lives spent dreaming of having eternity to do everything they wanted. They envied creatures they read about in books, creatures like me that kept their youth and roamed through centuries. What they didn't see was the ugly truth behind what we were. They were blind to all the suffering we went through while our physical bodies stayed the same, only memories of the pain left behind haunting our dreams.

And there wasn't even a scar to show for it.

3

Only memories.

Snatching my hand away, I tightened my fist and used the sharp bite of my nails to bring me out of that dark hole filled with misery. Nothing good ever came from dwelling on the past. Yet ... darting my gaze across the lights below us, I couldn't help the sigh that escaped me. I wished I was down there with them. I wished I belonged to their world instead of the hellish nightmare mine was. It was difficult to swallow the lump clogging my throat while my lashes fluttered to get rid of the burn behind my eyes. I would not cry. Looking back, I hadn't cried for years, and I had no intention to start now. No, I had a job to do.

"You need to move," Veronica mumbled as she turned to face me, her brown eyes full of pity. My lips pressed in a firm line of displeasure, but I couldn't blame my friend for feeling sorry for me. I was an emotional, pathetic fool most days, and what I was sent here to do would be just another thing to add to my nightmares. "Don't do anything stupid, Brooklyn, I beg of you. Not now."

A lock of fire-red hair fell over my eye and I blew it up in frustration. It wasn't like I planned to do stupid things, though the word stupid was debatable depending which perspective one used to look at things, of course. I just had issues with blindly following orders. Personally, I couldn't say needing more information before you took someone's life was stupid, but what did I know? According to those that ruled over my life, not much obviously.

"Bee?" Veronica squeezed my knee and brought me back to the present. "I can do it—"

"No, I got this." I didn't allow her to finish the sentence. She had done enough to cover for my little rebellions. I handled the cages. Veronica wouldn't last a week.

Plus, I had a plan.

A stupid one, of course.

"Forty minutes until landing," my friend reminded me, staring over the seat in front of her as she flattened invisible wrinkles on her pencil skirt.

Leave it to Veronica to be dressed to the nines no matter the situation. The black skirt she wore was paired with a silky champaign colored blouse that complimented her pale skin and blonde hair. With six-inch heels and her long legs folded primly to the side, she was ready to be on the cover of a magazine, not in an economy seat on a flight to Chicago. Or next to someone like me who was covered from head to toe in black leather, including the boots covering my feet. My fire-red hair and eerily bright green eyes were the only color anyone would ever see on me. I liked my clothing to match my mood, and it had been as dark as it could get for so long I couldn't remember it ever being any different.

My body jerked forward when one of the children sitting behind me kicked at the back of my seat, throwing another tantrum when his mother told him to put his seatbelt on. The poor woman was hissing threats at the boy, but they did nothing to intimidate the kid, though her voice was trembling from either her need to cry or just plain anger, but I had no clue which. Blowing out a breath through pursed lips, I nudged Veronica so she would let me out, pretending I didn't see the old pervert across the aisle ogling her ass when she gracefully unfolded her body like a swan rising from sleep.

She reached her arms up, stretching and twisting slightly left and right, which always did the trick. There was not one person on the plane that didn't stare openmouthed at her beauty. As far as distractions went, I couldn't ask for a better one. Sliding out of my window seat and keeping my eyes in front of me, I headed out to the lavatories separating us from the business class. Veronica's drowsy *"Oops, oh dear, I think I'm dizzy"* was drowned by the rustling of clothing when everyone jumped out to help, including the two flight attendants who were practically running to come to her aid.

My feet kept moving forward.

The red curtain wavered slightly as if someone was moving behind it just as I neared the door of the bathroom I was pretending I wanted to use. The plane dipped and we lost altitude again, but my steps didn't slow nor did my balance suffer from it. If anyone noticed, I wasn't aware of them. I kept getting closer to my goal. *You can do this. There is nothing to fear,* I reminded myself just as I reached for the curtain.

The thick fabric was yanked back before I touched it.

"You are not fine." It was the same flight attendant from earlier, her eyes narrowed on me in suspicion as she gripped the curtain in a tight-knuckled fist.

I didn't slow down.

My boots ate up the space between us, and she took a step back as if startled by my advance while she filled her lungs with air like she was about to tell me off or maybe even scream. Using my speed, I was next to her before she had time to process what was happening. I covered her mouth with one hand while pulling the curtain closed with the other. Left in the tight confines between the metal drawers behind her and me in front of her, her eyes bugged out, her nostrils flaring as she panted in fear. Lowering my face to hers, I allowed my lips to curl just enough so she could see the tips of my fangs. Her heart was hammering so hard I could feel it under my palm on her face. Such fragile creatures, humans were.

"Sleep," I whispered, taking hold of her upper arm when her eyes rolled to the back of her head.

Not a great plan, but it'd have to do. By the time she woke, she wouldn't remember what was reality and what was a dream. A perk no one but Veronica knew I had. Compelling people with your voice was a myth from human stories, and it was one that everyone laughed about.

I didn't laugh about it.

I was hiding it so I could keep my life.

Loosing precious time, I placed the woman in one of the seats in the tight place designated for the flight attendants before straightening and staring at the second curtain that would take me to the business class.

A throat cleared from somewhere in front of it and paper crinkled when the page of a book was flipped over. Behind me voices were overlapping, and among them I heard Veronica's assurances that she was okay, but they weren't very convincing, even to me. The girl was good when putting on the charm.

I slid through the curtain, my gaze darting over the top of the chairs until it stopped on the third row. He looked just like the rest of the humans, apart from two things that made him stand out: his steady heartbeat and the way his sweaty palm gripped the hand rest a tad too tight. Also, the stench of a shifter seared the inside of my nose so much my eyes watered from it. Ignoring the curious glances from those I passed, I walked up to him and crouched next to his seat, pretending I knew him by placing a hand over his forearm.

"If you make any sudden moves, I will kill you before you have a chance to blink."

Smiling sweetly, I watched his eyes widen in shock before bulging in horror when he saw my fangs. His dark, terrified gaze dropped to the pendant nestled on my throat —a symbol that made me someone's property and that was the same red color as my hair—and I watched a drop of sweat slide down the temple of his blanched face. His body trembled with the need to stand up and attack. Broad shouldered and easily over six feet, he was a male in his prime left to quake in front of a female he could break in half if given a chance. Well, any other female but me, that was.

It broadened my smile.

"You will walk with me back there." I jerked my head to the side and pointed at the extended area where I left the flight attendant. "One wrong twitch of a muscle and this plane will land with only corpses occupying it. Yours will be among them."

He lifted a shaking hand, spearing his fingers through the mass of curls sitting on top of his head. The stench of the sweat that had his shirt sticking to his body was burning my nostrils, but he blinked fast a few times before swallowing thickly and nodding his head. There was no mistaking the defeat in his eyes. Pushing up, he stood at the same time as I lifted off my crouch, my head reaching just slightly above his shoulder. My cocked eyebrow was enough for him to sigh and get moving without trying his luck. There was a good reason I was sent after him. We both knew he couldn't win.

Not with a monster like me.

The moment we were both crammed in the tight confines, I yanked the curtain closed, the sound making him flinch and face me with his knees slightly bent. Ignoring his fear, I strained to hear if Veronica was still entertaining her audience, and my own knees buckled in relief when I heard her soft chuckle.

I startled the male by taking a fistful of his shirt and yanking his face close to mine. "Can you shift here?"

"Wha-what …" he stuttered, but I didn't have time to wait for him to get his head out of his ass.

"Can you shift?" He kept gaping at me, so I shook him to get his brain online and glared at him. "The Syndicate is sending their regards, asshole. Will you shift, or will you die here?"

"I've done nothing …" When a muscle jumped in my jaw, he shrunk back and pressed his back to the metal drawers. "I can shift." His gravelly voice shook, the confusion in his deep brown eyes almost comical. Only, there was nothing funny about the situation for either of us.

"I will need you to shift and stay in the cargo area with the rest of the animals on board until you are transferred to the unclaimed baggage. A human will come to claim you there and take you to a safe house where you will stay as long as it takes. For the rest of your life if need be, do you understand? If you don't, we are both as good as dead." When he heard he wasn't going to die tonight, he almost dropped on his knees as his legs gave out on him. I had to hold him up by the flimsy fabric of his shirt while he nodded with gusto. "Hey." Hissing under my breath, I jerked him upright. "Look at my face and remember it as good as you remember your own. The time will come when I will need a favor. I will find you and you will do what I ask. Am I clear?"

"Of course … anything … please …"

"Shift."

I had to take a step back when he instantly obeyed, and between one breath and the next a gray wolf was pinning his ears while snarling at me where the male should've been. It tucked its tail when I bared my fangs at him. Keeping him in sight from the corner of my eye, I opened the latched door to the cargo area and he bolted down like his ass was on fire. I felt like my soul was in flames from the need to go down there and join him, too. Closing it, I stiffened for what I was about to do, but they left me no choice. I would not kill a creature like me just because they told me to do it. Not if I could help it.

Sticking my head out through the curtain, I crooked my finger at the first person who turned their head to see who was coming out. A human in his sixties with unassuming features, his receding hairline making the top of his head shine in the low light of the plane took the bait.

"Come." The human got up and joined me, keeping his watery blue eyes pinned on my face. *He doesn't have that much longer to live*, I convinced myself.

Acid burned the back of my throat.

"This will not hurt," I promised him as I closed the distance between us.

My shoulders were thrown back and my head lifted high when I joined Veronica back at our seats. Sliding in, I settled into my window seat, my distant and unseeing eyes looking through the glass. She shifted slightly next to me, that small movement speaking louder than if she shouted at me.

"It's done," I told the window, not daring to look at her.

A scream from ahead of us pierced the silent air of the plane, and it was followed by one of the flight attendants yelling for a doctor. Not that anyone could save the human now. My hand fisted in my lap.

"It had to be done." Veronica sighed, sinking back in her seat in relief.

"Yes." My heart did a painful pump against my ribs once before resuming its natural slow rhythm. "Where the Syndicate is concerned … this had to be done."

Good thing she had no idea what *this* was.

For both of our sakes, I'd make sure the Council never found out exactly what I had done either.

Chapter Two

The sound of my footsteps as the heel of my boots clicked on the tiled floor echoed around me and bounced off the high, vaulted ceilings and walls. The marble, oak wood, and extravagant accents decorating the large mansion stood in contrast to the portraits of stern, cruel faces glaring at me from the walls. The moment anyone stepped foot through the ornate double doors into the long open foyer they were transported to some eighteenth century royal house with only one thing missing: there were no butlers or maids there. What we had was soulless killers dressed in tactical pants with their torsos bare as they stood still like statues along the walls and waited for anyone to breathe wrong. They'd strike like vipers that had been starved to death.

Maybe they were.

One might say the Syndicate loved staying in the past between the interior of the place they called home and the gladiator-type goons guarding it inside and out. With great effort, I kept my body relaxed and graceful as if I didn't have a worry in the world, the weight of my dagger on my left thigh comforting me and giving me courage not to flick my gaze to see if they were watching me. I had more worries than there were stars in the sky, but who was counting? As long as I was the only one that knew about my little *plans,* all was good.

For now.

A deep belly laugh came from the slightly opened door of the chamber, as they liked to call it. Two goons were manning it while standing with their arms folded at their backs as they stared straight ahead. The one on the right had a bad burn covering half of his face that was still in the healing process, and I couldn't help but wonder what he had done to deserve that. We didn't have to do much around here to be punished, per se. All we had to do was be at the wrong place at the wrong time. I must've been staring at his face because a deep growl rumbled in his chest and he glared at me. I jerked my gaze away from him and locked it on the slightly open door just as I stopped a foot away from them. It took everything in me not to wipe my sweaty palms on the leather of my pants.

"I'm here to report." My even, emotionless tone silenced the hum of voices coming from the other side of the damn door.

Left standing for a lot longer than necessary, I resisted the urge to turn around and leave. If I could just keep walking for days, I might go so far away that I'd never have to see any of them again. Wishful thinking, but they couldn't stop me from dreaming. Just as I stupidly was about to do that, my name was called with an invitation to enter.

I took a step.

"Brooklyn, darling. I didn't think I would see you back so soon." The arrogant voice coming from right behind me made me falter.

"No need to mingle around when the job is done." Turning slowly to face him, my fist clenched out of my control. The goons didn't miss the move, either, but they gave me a break by raising their stares without a word. "Johnathan, I'd say it's nice to see you again but that would be a lie." My genuine smile made a line form between his perfectly styled eyebrows.

His pristine white shirt was perfectly molded to his upper body, the top two buttons open to reveal the blood-red pendant nestled there. With his hands tucked in the pockets of his black dress pants, he stood watching me with his head cocked to the side. Not too broad shouldered, Johnathan had a lean body that had fooled many to test his strength. He was thinner than most but deadly as a snake. The male would smile sweetly and honey would be pouring out of his mouth a second before he struck like a viper and ended someone's life.

He was also Veronica's lover.

"Still playing hard to get I see." Long, graceful fingers lifted to his honey blond hair, smoothing the few longer curls back while his black eyes were pinned on my face.

"Veronica didn't come with you?" Pretending he hadn't spoken, I even looked around him as if searching for her. "Let me guess, she was still doing her hair and makeup. So vain that girl. Am I right?"

"For the life of me I don't understand why she allows you to speak to her like that." Staring down his nose at me made him look uglier than he needed to be. He was a fine looking male if it wasn't for his personality. The moment he opened his mouth his good looks were flushed right down the toilet. I never understood what Veronica saw in him.

"She's my friend, and that's what friends do." Talking slowly as if he was dumb, I leaned forward as if I was about to tell him a secret. He followed suit subconsciously, which made me grin internally. "You should try getting one of those. But no one likes a kiss ass, do they?"

Johnathan's mouth twisted in anger as I spanned on my heel and pushed the door open. His hand flattened between my shoulder blades, making him look like he was good-naturedly guiding me inside. The strained smile plastered on his face was comical, but my own gloating one slipped when my eyes found three displeased stares glued to me from across a long table.

"I believe there was a good reason you kept us waiting, Brooklyn." Isaiah slanted his eyes, and the glint there told me he would kill me without batting an eye if I said a word wrong.

Jet black hair was tied in a low ponytail at the base of his head and his red lips stood out stark against his white skin. His black robes folded over his body in layers, allowing the red piping to stand out like droplets of blood being sprinkled across the fabric. It matched the attire of the other two males in the room, who were watching me with equally bloodthirsty stares. Frozen in their mid-thirties, the three Council members could've been ruling over Hollywood while being admired by men and women alike around the world. They were so perfect it almost hurt to gaze at their beauty, but that was only skin deep. They were all angelic on the outside, but there were no bigger monsters if you looked inside. Instead of admiration, they chose fear as their reason for existing. Older than dirt, all three were what supernaturals were afraid of. It was very simple in their world.

The Council of the Syndicate understood only power.

And you'd better not have more than them.

If you did, those like me were sent to fix the problem.

"Johnathan wanted to join me, Sire." Bowing my head in submission that rubbed me wrong on so many levels, I kept my voice soft and meek. "I meant no disrespect. I thought it will please you."

"What of the scum?" Frederic, sprawled on the right of Isaiah, flicked a lock of his white blonde hair over his shoulder as he trailed his fingers over the arm of the woman swaying on her feet next to him. Red rivulets flowed down her arm, thick droplets splattering the top of the table below it. His lips were stained with her blood, and I watched his tongue poke out to lick it off.

A sharp pain stabbed me at the center of my chest, and it almost doubled me over.

"Dead." The strain in my choked words couldn't be helped, and the asshole gave me a malicious grin, all fangs and teeth as if he could feel the phantom pain in my own arm throbbing.

"Excellent." Frederic purred, sinking his fangs in the woman's arm again without looking away from me. The human didn't have much longer to live.

I looked at her then. Her face was so pale it was graying on the edges of her cheeks, which stood high on a once-pretty face. Her blue eyes were unfocused and sunken on her expressionless face, and her thick hair was flattened to her skull from sweat. Her naked body was trembling and swaying while she blinked fast and tried to clear her vision. I willed her to see me, and when her gaze cleared for that one moment, I internally whispered a promise from the bottom of my soul that I would remember her face. Just like I remembered the others brought to this hell where they will die. Given as an offering for peace, or to pay off a debt, every human knew stepping in that they would not be getting out alive. It could've just been my imagination, but I thought her cracked lips lifted slightly at the corners in a sad, grateful smile before her hand went limp and she dropped in a heap on the floor. Frederic released her arm in disgust, wiping his mouth with the back of his hand.

I glared.

I couldn't help it.

"Is there a problem, dear?" The sweet tone of his voice did not match the arched eyebrow daring me to say anything that would dig my own grave.

"Not at all … Sire." I wished to remove the smirk off his face with my dagger.

But I just stood there.

"Perhaps I could talk some sense into her, Sire," the kiss-ass next to me offered casually. "It seems our Brooklyn still struggles with obedience and manners." I stiffened and my jaw clenched when he chuckled.

He still hadn't removed his hand from my back.

"Remove your hand if you'd like to keep it." Looking forward, my words were so soft that his arm dropped before I was finished talking.

"No need for that, Johnathan." My chest stopped squeezing my lungs when I heard those words. "Your father would be so proud, child." Samir, the third and last member, spoke in his calm deep voice.

My eyes darted to the portrait hanging away from all others that covered the mansion. This one was above the massive fireplace that took up almost an entire wall of the room. The same pale skin and electric green eyes stared back at me from a face resembling mine so much it couldn't be mistaken whose child I was. His black hair was the only difference between us. My red hair came from my mother, just adding to the freakshow I turned out to be among my kind.

"I do try not to soil his name and reputation, Sire." Which was true … to a point.

I didn't know much about him, only that he belonged to the Syndicate just like I did now. Or so I was told, which didn't explain why his portrait was sitting in this chamber. They told me he died in the war we had centuries ago when the rest of the supernaturals banded together in hopes to kill all of the Syndicate. My father's portrait was placed in this room to show him honor because he lost his life to protect the Council members.

I didn't believe a word of it.

According to the tales they spun, we won the war, and from that day forward even the slightest rise in power was punishable by death. They fancied themselves to be rulers and lawmakers. What the Syndicate actually depicted was the same as what the Mafia was for the humans.

Black Hand was what the rest of the supernatural world called us.

They never said it to our face.

"We should celebrate." Blinking fast, I looked away from my father's painting to see Isaiah watching me intently. "For a job well done." The smile didn't reach his eyes.

My nod was slow and wary because my mind was racing through ways I could get out of it. The three ancients were watching the internal war play out in my mind, but they grinned the moment they saw defeat in my eyes. There would be no getting out of it, though I knew any kind of celebration would be more like a massacre in this place. My deep sigh only widened their smiles.

"You are free to go, Brooklyn." Isiah twirled his hand as if shooing me off. "Do not wander too far. The party will commence in a few hours. Understood?"

"Yes, Sire." I hated the fact that they knew me too well.

"Johnathan will accompany you, yes?" Frederic was lucky I didn't jump at him and scratch his eyes out.

"I will attend alone." Jutting my chin out, I glared at him. "Or not at all."

"You must accept—" Isiah started, scowling at my glare, but Samir lifted a hand to stop the threats I could see coming.

"Alone it is, child." His caramel complexion stuck out like a sore thumb among the other two pale faces, giving him a more approachable appearance. It was just a façade, but it worked, nonetheless. "You shall sit next to me, yes?"

"Of course, Sire. It would be my honor." The words tasted like acid on my tongue.

Johnathan's face looked like he drank the acid I felt rising in my throat.

I gave Samir a genuine smile for that alone.

"Now, get out of my face," Isiah snarled baring his fangs at me, all pretense of a civilized being gone in the blink of an eye.

"As you wish, Sire." Flipping my hand with flourish, I bowed before whirling around and bolting out of the room.

Samir's guffaw echoed behind me, the sound drowning out all the cursing spilling from Isaiah's lips. I had no doubt that I'd pay for that little tantrum later. But it was so worth it to leave that kiss-ass Johnathan inside a room with a pissed-off Isiah. If I was lucky, he might have a missing eye tonight.

How was that for a celebratory gift?

My cheeks hurt from how hard I was smiling as I hurried to find Veronica and warn her about what was coming. Because when the Syndicate was celebrating, the rest of the world mourned.

I needed to be ready for anything.

Chapter Three

The industrial part of the city was a favorite place of mine, and I went there often to get away from all the crazy that was my life. Reaching up for the fire escape, I yanked the metal railing down and jumped on it while it was still rolling toward the ground. The clinking of my boots bounced off the alley and a cat screeched from one of the banged-up dumpsters in the narrow space. My heart skipped a beat at the feral sound and a nervous chuckle burst through my lips. With my face tilted up, I kept climbing until I reached the roof of the abandoned warehouse.

Debris, rotten leaves from the tall tree on one side of the structure, and who knew what else littered the top of the warehouse. I was picking my way around it all and flicking a few things away with the toes of my boots. The vents and air conditioning units were sticking out of the flat structure like humps on a camel, so I had to weave around them, and when I did the city came to life before my eyes. When I reached my spot, the place where I came to just breathe, it felt like coming home. Or at least that was what coming home should feel like.

I didn't know for sure.

Lights twinkled from across the tall buildings that were rising up high as if reaching to touch the moon. The honking of cars and the buzz of the city was as clear to me as if I was standing in the thick of it while the human world moved around me. Curling my knees to my chest, I wrapped my arms around them and took a deep breath, my eyes closing from the peace of it all. Even the stench was soothing somehow.

It didn't smell like corpses.

Or blood.

Or metal cages …

A shudder made me rub my hands over my upper arms to ward off the chill seeping into my bones. The past was behind me and I had to keep it there. Thinking about those nightmares would drive any person insane.

The rolling of a pebble stiffened my shoulders.

"It's just me." Those hushed words were as loud as a shout to any of my kind, but I never told her that. "Why on earth you always want to meet here is beyond me, Brooklyn. It stinks like a shithouse."

"Good to see you too, Alice." I turned to look at her over my shoulder, biting on my lip so I didn't laugh when she stumbled over a rock that somehow found its way onto this roof.

Alice was human. She was also an animal rights activist that had the balls to stand up to me one night when I was attacked by a shifter. The poor woman thought I was trying to hurt the dog—though it wasn't a dog at all, but I had no way in hell explaining that to her. I wasn't sure who was more confused, me or the damn shifter, when she planted herself between us and shook her fist at me like a ninety-year-old grandma telling off a child. I also believed her mouth was foaming in anger more than the wolf's behind her. When it came to animals, you did not mess with Alice Green. The woman would tear you apart with her bare hands.

It gave me an idea.

The same idea that I was well aware would cost me my life one of these days.

Cursing up a storm under her breath, she lifted her head and pushed the thick frames of her glasses up her nose. Her dark hair fell over her shoulders in waves all the way to her lower back, and her thin frame was covered in a long flowing tie-dye dress. Strands of crystals clinked as they swayed around her neck and wrists while she tattered and stumbled her way to me.

"What was so damn important that I had to come meet you now?" Plopping next to me, she wrinkled her nose. "Man, it stinks here."

"Your nose is stuck in animal shit all day and this stinks?"

"That's different."

"How?"

"What did you need?"

That's one thing I loved about Alice. The woman had no idea who I was so she talked to me like I should be the one afraid of her. After that little debacle with the shifter—who ended up being leashed and dragged to the canal where Alice works, much to my delight—the human decided that she would teach me how to respect all life. What she actually taught me was how I could screw the Syndicate and not have to actually kill the supernaturals they sent me to dispose of.

She was also the one human who didn't scream bloody murder when they saw me. To Alice Green, I was simply Brooklyn, the redhead who had no respect for life unless it was a human one. If she only knew …

"Did you pick up the unclaimed baggage?" Ignoring her indignant huff, I watched her face.

"Of course I picked it up, just as you knew I would." Folding both arms across her chest, she looked at me over her glasses. "I still don't know where you find all these huge animals. If they weren't so well behaved, I would've bet my life that the huge dogs were wolves."

"They are mixed breeds, and no one wants them because of their size. You said you'd take care of them." Shrugging a shoulder and acting like I didn't care one way or another, I rolled my gaze over the buildings across from us. "If it's too much for you I can find someone else—"

"I didn't say it was too much." The tone of her voice told me I'd insulted her, which had been my intention. "They are beautiful. The one I just picked up is very well trained, too. He sits, stays… and listen to this, he even rolled when I told him to."

The excited clap of her hands covered the strangled sound escaping my throat. I almost choked on my own tongue while she grinned at me with so much pride on her face. The crazy human made a powerful shifter roll like a pet. I guess I'd have to rethink asking that one to repay the favor. He might be rolling now because he was still afraid for his life, but after a day or two with Alice, he'd attack me the second he lays eyes on me.

"What the …You did what?" I stuttered, gaping at her.

She nodded so hard her glasses slid all the way to the tip of her nose. "He rolled. It was so exciting." Alice gushed, pushing her frames up with her forefinger before smoothing her wild hair back away from her face. "I might keep this one, you know. He looks like he will be a good guard dog and great company."

"No." My harsh snap made her deflate like a balloon being popped. "Alice, you and I had a deal. You pick up the ones I find, and then you release them into one of the reservations. You promised." Reminding her of all the promises she threw at me when we made this deal was always a good strategy.

"Fine." Pouting like a child, she wiggled to get more comfortable on the cold concrete. "He would be better off with me than alone roaming the reservation, though. You know that as well as I do."

If he was actually a dog, I had no doubt. He would've lived like a royalty. But my reason for releasing them into one of the reservations was a good one.

Shamans.

The native tribes had plenty of shamans practicing their craft, and the energy they created prevented any of the Atua to step foot on their lands. I never understood the mechanics of it, but I didn't really care. The Syndicate would never find the ones I'd let live as long as they were there. Shifters were also welcomed among the tribes. They called them skin walkers, and they were fiercely protected. By keeping the shifters hidden, those shamans protected my life as well.

"I know, Alice." Reaching, I squeezed her forearm in reassurance. "But the ones I ask you to take to the reservations have too much wild in them. They need to be free. You want them to be free and happy, don't you?"

"I know." She made a face and pursed her lips. "He is just so sweet."

If the Council wanted him dead, there was nothing sweet about him.

"We will get you a dog." *A real one*, I added in my head. One that wouldn't try to find me when he shifted back, and one that wouldn't rip Alice's throat out for making him roll. "I'll find one for you."

"Right. Is that why you asked me to come?" Tugging her dress closer to her body, she glanced around. "I could've told you all of that on the phone. I don't like this place."

"We don't talk about these things over the phone."

"True, all those government leeches will hear every word we say. They'll probably raid my kennel, too." Her eyes darted around as if a swat team was going to jump out of the shadows. Alice was a bit of a conspiracy theorist. She didn't know that one of the creatures she was scared would come take over humanity was sitting right next to her. On a good note, at least I wasn't an alien, right?

"I just wanted to make sure you have him and that you will release him tonight."

"I was getting ready to head that way when you called." Lifting up, she dusted the back of her dress with short, nervous swats. "And Brooklyn?"

I looked up and my chest got tight from the unsure, vulnerable look on her face. Unable to speak through my constricted throat, I jerked my chin in question to prompt her to ask whatever had her making the expression she wore on her face. She might be a little peculiar, but she was one of the kindest people I had met in my long life.

"One of these days, we can … you know … have a cup of coffee, or I don't know … tea? In a café, like normal people. Because I kind of think of you as a friend, and I think friends do that. Well, I know they do that—" She cut herself off with a groan. "I sound like an idiot. I blabber when I'm nervous. So?" I could tell she was holding her breath.

I was ready to say, "You don't want to hang around me," but I simply couldn't. There was so much hope in her eyes it was choking the life out of me. Even though I knew it was the worst decision along a string of bad choices I'd made recently, I found myself nodding at her. The smile that brightened her face turned it to something truly beautiful.

"That's great, we can do it this week—"

A scream ripped the quiet night around us and I was on my feet guarding Alice with my body before she had time to move. Her whispered "What the fuck" was drowned by another terror-filled screech that pebbled my skin.

"Stay here." When she didn't answer, I turned to stare at her. "Alice!" Her eyes were thick with fear when they jerked to my face. "Stay here."

When she started nodding like a bobblehead, I spun on my heel and almost threw myself down the fire escape. The scream came from nearby, so like a hound I lifted my nose and followed the stench of fear and terror not even half a block down the road. With dread weighing heavily in my stomach, I reached the lump on the corner and lowered next to it, my gaze darting around me in search of whoever was there. Because they were still near. I could feel their eyes burning a hole through my skin. What was confusing was the faint scent of a shifter lingering in the air, but it must've been from Alice being near me since it was there one second and gone the next.

My hand found no pulse on the already-cooling skin of the human's wrist. When I finally looked down, the horror-filled eyes were wide and unseeing, while the mouth of the young woman was open in a silent scream. For just a moment I dared to hope something else had killed her. Until

I saw that her neck was chewed up the same way my arms use to be. I was so careful, yet I'd made a crucial mistake. Someone must've followed me here, and this was a message that they had me in the palm of their hand.

"Is she dead?" The question made me squeeze my eyes shut and pray for any help the fates or gods would give me. Because I had a bigger problem than the dead woman at my feet.

The Syndicate knew about Alice.

Chapter Four

"You are going to be late."

Anger and relief mixed into one when I saw Johnathan leaning on one of the lounge chairs the moment I walked through the front doors. It couldn't have been him at the city, not if I went by the way he was dressed and the leering look in his eyes. If he was the one who followed me, there would be victory written all over his dumb face.

"So I'll be late." Shrugging a shoulder, I kept my gaze pinned on the wide rounding staircase to keep up the pretense of the nonchalance I didn't feel. "I'm used to punishment. You, on the other hand, might rethink hanging around me like you're the narrator of my life. They might rearrange your pretty face."

Taking the stairs two at a time and pretending I didn't hear his snide remarks, I had just about enough energy to keep my heartbeat steady. After accompanying Alice back to her home and making sure no one followed us there, it took all of four minutes and twenty seconds for me to haul ass and get back to the mansion. That left no more than five to get ready and show up in the hall where the Council expected me to be right on the dot.

I was going to be late.

"One of these days you'll have to give in, Brooklyn, and forgive me for everything because it was all for your own good." Johnathan called out, and I stopped at the top of the staircase to look down at him. For a second there he even looked sincere, but then he opened his mouth. "You know as well as I do that we'd make the perfect match to take over parts of the Syndicate's empire. The Council knows it, too."

"The only match I'm thinking about is the one I'll be lighting over your corpse if you get anywhere near me, Johnathan. Now that will be perfect."

His furious expression made me feel a little better, and I couldn't keep away the small smile that tilted my lips. I had a problem killing people for no given reason, but the Syndicate life is all I'd ever known. I'd have no problem at all killing him. I'd actually enjoy it, come to think of it. With that image firmly in place, I pushed the door of my room open and stepped inside.

"I have everything ready, just take those horrible clothes off." Veronica turned away from my dresser holding a brush in one hand and what looked like a string in the other.

She heard at least half of the conversation at the staircase.

"Veronica ..."

"Don't worry about it, Bee. He is an idiot. I know it, you know it ... Hell, the entire community knows it." Waving me off, she wiggled the brush at me. "Come on, you don't have to be late by much."

"You will be late, too." My words were muffled from the shirt I tugged over my head at the same time as I kicked my boots off. It had the same odor I smelled on the roof of the warehouse and my nose wrinkled. Shockingly, Johnathan didn't say anything about that. "I'm not a child. I can dress myself."

"Have you met you?" My friend's face was twisted in horror, and I couldn't stop the bark of laughter that escaped me. "They'll kick us both out of there if I let you dress yourself."

"We can hope?" Her tinkling laughter joined mine and we both sighed. "That's a pipe dream."

"Here." She waved the string she had in her hand just as I kicked the pile my leather pants made around my ankles. "Put this on and hurry."

"What the hell is that?" Taking it between two fingers, I lifted it closer to my face when she smacked my arm.

"Something you will be wearing, so put it on."

"Is this underwear?" My eyes were bugging out as I flung the stupid thing at her chest. "That's some shit you'd wear, not me. Pass. Next!" I was turning away to grab a pair of my boxer briefs when something shiny in her arms got my attention from the corner of my eye, so I did a double take. "Oh, hell no. Get that thing away from me."

Veronica was dressed in skin-tight silk that pooled around her feet as she walked. The pale blue color of her dress made her look almost ethereal, like a dream come to life. The diamonds twinkled where they dangled from her ears and peeked through the smooth strands of her blonde hair, which was falling like a waterfall over her shoulders. No one would think much of it because that was how she always looked. Almost as if you had to reach out and touch her to assure yourself she was real.

What she had in her arms was also silk by the looks of it, the shiny emerald color almost the same shade as my eyes.

My friend was cradling it like it was something precious, and I was waiting for the war inside me as I internally screamed in horror while wanting to laugh out loud at the absurdity.

She wanted me to dress like her but we had one problem: I was not Veronica.

I'd never be her, and that was the reason I loved her so much. She was everything that was good in my world. Everything that I would never be. It made me so protective of her, to the point that I would burn this place down if a hair was missing from her head. Some of the emotions must've shown on my face because she cleared her throat as she stepped closer, and when she did I could see her eyes were brimming with unshed tears.

"Trust me, Bee." She took a deep breath and blew it out slowly. "Something doesn't feel right around here. It's as if they expect you to do something, or they are hoping you will. We are going to be late anyway. Let's make it look like we at least put in some kind of effort. Please? And when we have a moment I'd like to talk to you about...things" she swallowed thickly. "I heard some things, but not here, and not now."

Unable to speak through the lump in my throat, I simply nodded once and started putting on what she handed me. The damn string wedged itself in my ass, but I had such turmoil inside me that not even that could bother me. Goosebumps popped out all over my body when the silk slid down my arms and grazed my skin every time I slightly shifted. With clenched teeth, I stood while Veronica brushed my hair and left it lose around my face. I barely noticed her putting earrings on me, at least until she adjusted the pendant at the base of my throat.

"I wish you could see how beautiful you are, Bee." She

smoothed stray hairs like a mother would to a child, and I had to blink fast and look away.

"I don't want to look beautiful, Veronica. Threatening and intimidating works for me." When she rolled her eyes, I snorted. "Okay, a little unhinged, too."

"You got that one down pat." Snickering, she nudged me to put the hazardous-looking heels on.

"I'm going to break a leg." When I straightened and looked at the long mirror, not even I could say that Veronica didn't know what she was doing. My eyes paired with the dress were a deeper green, my hair was like flames flickering around my face and shoulders.

"They say break a leg for good luck." My gaze locked on hers when she came to stand behind me.

"Luck does not work in the Syndicate."

"No, but brains do." Her pointed, silver-painted nail tapped my temple. "And you have more than is good for you in that department." Taking hold of my shoulders, she turned me and pushed for me to start walking. "Let's go show those idiots what's it all about."

"I really don't feel like going." Grumbling, I allowed her to guide me from my room. The sound of the door closing behind us was like a nail to my head.

"I know, Bee. You'll be just fine." Linking our arms, she bumped her shoulder off mine. "But you'll have me there. The drama queen is always ready to take the spotlight. I got you."

"You shouldn't have to." Glancing at her sideways, I focused on getting enough air in my lungs. "You are more intelligent than all of them put together." The ungraceful snort coming from her made me stumble. She never made that sound.

"You know that and that's enough for me. It's you and

me, kid. I have absolutely nothing to prove to those fools." Her shoulders snapped back when we started descending the staircase, and I mimicked her posture like a monkey in a circus. Monkey did what monkey saw, only this one wobbled on the high heels. "Plus, it's easier to get away with a lot of things when they think you are dumb." Winking over her shoulder, Veronica plastered a smile on her face as she sped ahead of me.

If I did that, I would've probably broken my neck when I fell down the stairs.

People mulled around the mansion, most of them headed in the same direction I was. Curious eyes followed my every step, but I kept my chin up and my head held high. I didn't look at any of them. They all knew about me from the day I was born—the redheaded Atua. I was the only one of my kind with flame-red hair. Now they also knew me as the one that survived the cages. The only one who walked out of those pits of hell on her own two feet. The fact that I crawled out of there scratching my way out was something I hadn't told anyone. Not even Veronica, but I had a feeling she knew. The sharp ping in my chest snapped me out of those thoughts just as I neared the doors of the hall where Veronica was patiently waiting for me, and she was standing next to the kiss ass. She rushed her way down on purpose so they didn't see us coming together. My friend would go to great lengths to cover for me.

There was not one thing I wouldn't do for her, either.

"There you are, Brooklyn. Holy crap, you look amazing." If I wasn't talking to her a couple of minutes ago, even I would've believed we hadn't seen each other all night. "Johnathan darling, doesn't she look stunning?"

The look I gave the kiss ass dared him to say one word out of line in front of my friend. I would've walked inside that hall carrying his dead body like a bloody sacrifice to the gods. That might make the Council happy for sure. His startled blinking told me he received the message loud and clear.

"Indeed, she does, love." Wrapping an arm around her shoulders, he didn't look away from my glare. "Doesn't she always?"

"Johnathan." Joining them, I kept my eyes locked on his even when Veronica gave me a peck on the cheek. "How very not nice to see you."

The asshole laughed while I clenched my teeth. "Charming as always, Brooklyn." His intense gaze promised me retribution, and I looked forward to whatever it might be. "That mouth will get you in a lot of trouble."

"I'd love to say I like to hear all the bullshit coming out of your own mouth, but I don't want to keep the Council waiting." Shouldering my way between him and Veronica, I grabbed her arm and tugged her with me. "But that would be too many lies in one sentence, even for me."

Veronica chuckled under her breath, and my lips were twitching when we walked through the open double doors of the hall. I took two steps inside when my heart did a lurch and dropped to my feet, and I just knew all the blood had drained from my face. Samir leaned on one pillar smoothing his goatee with one hand and twirling his pendant between his fingers of the other. The look on his face was calculating and cunning, so intense that it sent chills crawling up and down my spine. My hand tightened painfully around Veronica's arm. I really needed to learn to keep my mouth shut, which was about the only thing the kiss ass was right about.

"Sire." Veronica rushed to my rescue, gushing at the Council member with batting eyelashes. "If I didn't know better, I would've thought they placed a statue of a god near the entrance."

Bile burned the back of my throat.

Samir didn't take those cunning eyes off me as he opened his arms to embrace Veronica. "Sire." My mumbled greeting left a lot to be desired.

"You clean up well, child." His smooth voice only added to my anxiety.

"I do try, Sire." Ducking my head, I wished I could be anywhere else but in the damn hall. "Apologies for being late."

"Not important, you are here now." His hand whirled in dismissal, but I knew it was important. Very important when he continued talking. "Let us find Frederic and Isaiah. They were looking forward to your appearance."

Veronica and I exchanged a look, and the events from earlier this night hit me like a punch to the head.

"Johnathan, you should join us as well." Samir spoke over my shoulder, and I had to swallow the lump the size of a fist in my throat.

This was bad.

This was really, really bad.

Chapter Five

The laughter and good-natured slapping of shoulders while cheerfully discussing random things contrasted drastically with the sunken faces of the humans whose naked bodies were stretched out on tables like some medieval feast. The only thing missing was the glistening glaze, which had been replaced by the cold sweat their fear blanketed their bodies with and the apple stuck in their mouths. They'd left their mouths free to hear their screams and pleading.

On numb legs, I followed Samir through the crowds that were parting in front of him with deep bows and reverent phrases. None of them could hide the glances they threw my way. Veronica's arm wrapped around mine was the only thing keeping me from bolting out of there. That and the kiss ass riding my tail at my back. It felt like I was being taken to a guillotine, and the smooth silk grazing my skin from the long dress was like blades nipping at my skin.

Saying I was on edge would've been the understatement of the century.

"She is here," Samir announced as he stepped to the

side, revealing the grotesque scene of the three raised chairs in the hall.

Samir's chair was empty, and I wished I could say the same for the other two. Isiah and Frederic had forgone the robes for this evening, sleeking their long hairs in matching ponytails at the base of their heads. Expensive looking fabric stretched across their wide shoulders, the form-fitting suits giving them a modern appearance their archaic ways lacked. When the two sets of eyes locked on my face, everything I was shrunk back in hopes I'd turn invisible. There was nothing but evil lurking there. Not a trace of anything but hunger for death and power.

Veronica's arm trembled around mine.

"Sires." My pathetic nod should've been insulting, but it only stretched their grins wider while they leered at me.

"Brooklyn," Isiah said my name like some inside joke I wasn't privy to. "Come join me." Shoving away the human peeing all over himself, he petted the armrest of his throne-like chair.

Insanity took over my brain.

"I gave my word to Samir to be his company tonight." My chin jutted out in defiance as I glared down my nose at him.

A horrifying smile curled Isiah's lips, leaving only the tips of his bloodstained fangs visible. It sent a torrent of panic through my bloodstream.

"I am sure he wouldn't mind," the asshole purred as he cocked an eyebrow at the Council member in question.

"By all means." Samir flung a hand to the side to show me where I needed to go so I could round the long table and obey Isiah.

My feet weighed a ton as I stepped around him. Ignoring Samir waving at someone to bring more chairs to the table, I kept my eyes trained in front of me. That was the only reason I didn't see the idiot coming to meet me halfway. When he blocked my path, I flinched, and that reaction made my blood pressure hit the roof.

"Sires, you never mentioned what a beauty little Brooklyn turned out to be." The male standing in my way looked familiar but not enough for me to place him as someone I'd seen often.

"Get out of the way before I make you." It was like having an out of body experience. I heard my voice, sure, but I hadn't consciously meant to say the words.

Veronica gasped.

The Council members chuckled.

"I think Brooklyn does not remember you, Noah." Frederic flicked his hand, indicating for the idiot to let me pass.

They outright laughed when I bumped my shoulder into his when he didn't get out of my way fast enough. I might've had to act meek and pretend I was submissive to the Council. That didn't mean I had to do the same for the rest of them. Killing without reason never sat well with me. When it came to survival, it was either me or them. Take a guess as to what I always chose.

Lowering myself gingerly on the armrest of Isaiah's chair, I had to bite the inside of my mouth to keep it shut when he petted my thigh. Through the silk it felt like he was touching my bare skin, and my nostrils flared in rage. Veronica's pleading eyes calmed the irrational thoughts of ripping his arm out and beating him with it. All the noise from the hall and the people moving around pretending they were not focused on the drama happening here faded to the background, along with the humans crying and pleading for their lives. In my world, I'd grown numb to those after a while. The same scent of a shifter drifted under my nose, and I turned to peer over my shoulder as I tried to pinpoint who it belonged to. I was so focused on finding him that I missed what Isaiah was saying.

The arrogant smirk on his face told me he thought his nearness made me flustered, so I gave him a tight smile. "I'm sorry, what?" Focusing on my breathing, I blinked at him stupidly.

"Noah is the one that fought alongside your father." My head jerked to the male in question, and I didn't miss the slight nervous shift his body made. His behavior brought up some red flags, but I didn't give it much thought. "He took over our security after your father was killed. The position makes him travel a lot, so you haven't seen him around much after your ... return."

That was a nice way of saying escaping the cages. The same cages they put me in for asking too many questions and refusing to blindly do their bidding. The curl of my lips matched Isaiah's this time, and hopefully it reminded him that since I'd done it once I could do it again. I made a decision a long time ago to not let them hold that over my head.

Feeling Veronica's stare on me, I flicked my gaze her way. A slight frown pulled at my eyebrows when she turned to look pointedly first at Noah and then at Johnathan, who sidled closer to the male. Frederic was telling Isaiah something that I totally ignored in my attempt to understand what she was trying to tell me. Is this what she wanted to tell me, that Noah was here and good buddies with the kiss ass? My mouth opened to say something that would make her come closer to me, and that was when all hell broke loose.

A scream silenced every sound in the entire mansion.

A grave made more noise than the hall.

Isiah jumped up from his chair, which sent it toppling back with me still perched on the armrest. The thin heels of my shoes lost contact with the floor and I sailed in the air backwards like I was on a rollercoaster ride. My stomach did backflips, too, before my back hit the ground and all the air was shoved out of my lungs.

It was chaos.

Shouts and snarls were louder than anything else as I shook my head to clear it. Scrambling around, I tried to stand up but my heel got caught in the silk of my dress. I tipped to the side as I realized the damn string pretending to be my underwear was cutting between my ass cheeks, which pissed me off, too. My ribs and shoulder protested from the impact as I flailed around like a fish out of water.

"This is why I don't wear fucking dresses." I hissed angrily at the stupid dress when a hand wrapped around my arm and hauled me up.

"We have a problem." Veronica panted next to me, her nails digging into the skin of my upper arm.

"No shit. What gave it away?" Jerking my arm out of her grip, I tried to assess the situation.

"Don't be an ass, Bee. We have a shitstorm happening."

Everyone was running out of the hall, pulling daggers and other weapons that glinted in the light of the swinging chandeliers. Naked, barely-alive humans huddled in groups in the corners trying to make themselves look as small as possible. An explosion shook the foundations of the mansion and pitched me sideways into Veronica. We both stumbled while reaching blindly for any sort of support.

"What the fuck is going on?" I expected many things tonight, but this was not one of them.

"Someone attacked the mansion." The awe in her voice was reflected on my face.

"Who in their right mind would attack the Syndicate at home?"

"I know, right?" Her nervous laugh was contagious, so I joined her. "Listen ..." When she paused for too long, I turned to give her a quick glance. "Do you think maybe it has something to do with your jobs lately, the ones that were done but not really done?" Chewing on her lower lip, she watched me with a sheepish look. My stomach dropped. "I knew what you were doing. That's why I was hell bent on coming with you. In case we need to do a coverup or something."

"Veronica, I ..." Lost for what to say, all I could do was sigh and scrub a hand over my face like that would everything better.

"I don't need an explanation, Bee. I just want you to know I'm proud of you." Tears shimmered in her eyes. "Do you think that may have something to do with this?"

"No way." All those shifters were safely in the reservations. Hopefully they'd stay there for a very long time, too. "I have no idea what this is, but I'm about to find out."

"Where the hell do you think you are going?" She grabbed for me, clawing at my arms to stop me from leaving our safe place near the wall. The two of us were as pathetic as the humans.

"If someone is attacking the Syndicate"—Glancing around to make sure no one was listening, I leaned closer to her—"I'm going to help them."

Her wide-eyed stare was comical on her, but I didn't stay long enough to enjoy my friend being shocked speechless. Kicking off my damn heels and lifting my dress in two fistfuls, I darted across the hall, my gaze focused on the open doors. My bare feet slid on the smooth tiles when I entered, the billowing smoke filling up the mansion. At first, I thought it was from the explosion, but soon I found out it was something entirely different. People who were chatting in friendly manner a few minutes ago were now trying to kill each other. Everyone in attendance for the celebration was fighting among themselves, their fancy clothing turning into shreds from blades and fangs ripping at it.

My head was getting foggy while I stood just on the edges of the smoke, and I had to shake it to clear out the irrational urge for violence. Taking a step back, I held my breath while ripping at silk in my fists. Bunching up the smooth fabric from my now mini-dress, I shoved it over my nose and mouth while trying to make out anything in the foggy hallways. Someone was shouting from up ahead and telling everyone not to breathe whatever was released inside the mansion. Atua didn't have to breathe to survive, but holding our breath would make us sluggish and slow us down considerably, so we made it a habit just like the humans.

The two males throwing punches at each other closest to me stumbled back, and I had to duck so I didn't get hit in the head. One of them jostled my body with his spin kick and the fabric slipped through my fingers to fall on the floor. Dropping on my hands and knees, I crawled forward while snatching the silk the whole time. That was when the scent of a shifter hit me stronger than ever. The thick smoke was lingering and curling a couple of feet above ground, which made the air bearable. My head swiveled as I looked around, my nose lifted as high as I dared to find the direction of the smell. The scent didn't give the shifter away, but his shoes definitely did. Down here among all the fancy high heels and shiny shoes, a pair of sneakers stood out as if screaming at me to notice them. The feet moved further inside the mansion, so stuffing the silk over my nose and mouth, I jumped up and followed on their heels.

My mind raced as fast as the adrenaline pumping

through my veins. How did I tell whoever it was that I wanted to help before they attacked and tried to kill me? Did I just say, "Hey, you need some help?" Or maybe it would be, "Let me help. I want to mess them up as much as you do.' Ducking, twisting, and turning, I followed the shifter up the staircase leading to the rooms. My heart stopped when a dagger flew in front of my face to sink into the wall parallel to my head. None of them would be alive when all this was over if they kept throwing weapons blindly. I had to give it to the shifter. It was a genius plan that I should've thought of sooner myself.

Reaching the top of the stairs after jumping over dead bodies and heads rolling like balls across the floors, I realized the smoke was thinner here, too. I thought I heard my name being called, but I couldn't see a polar bear gunning for me if I tried in all the gray below. Knowing my luck, it was probably the kiss ass using the chaos to kill me and get me out of his way finally. A shrill scream made me jump a foot off the ground, and that was when I realized I'd been wrong. Johnathan hadn't been calling from below. Not when he popped out of nowhere and faced off with the shifter I'd been follower.

The very male shifter, at that.

His back was to me, his wide shoulders stretching his thin t-shirt an inch from its life. His jeans were pulled snug over powerful thighs as he braced himself for Johnathan's attack. Whatever he was, he sure didn't smell like a wolf, which he confirmed the second sharp, long claws sprouted from his fingers. A feline then. Muscles bunched and jumped under the fabric of his shirt when he crouched and taunted Johnathan to make the first move.

But I knew the kiss ass.

He would neither fight fair nor put himself in the position to have a hair ruffled on his head. Johnathan was going to fight dirty, and the shifter was going to die. For some stupid reason, the urge to not let that happen reared its head inside me. Veronica's voice echoed in my head. "You can't save them all. Why make life harder for yourself?" But she was wrong. One by one I might not save them all, but I'd save as many as I could. So, the moment Johnathan tensed to do whatever he had planned, I made my move.

I rammed the shifter from behind, taking both of us down rolling on the floor until we hit one of the walls. Johnathan's enraged scream echoed through the space, but thankfully the smoke was reaching the top and now hid us from view. A hand as large as my head with wicked claws passed an inch from my nose when I jerked back to avoid being skewered. Not wasting time talking—mostly so the kiss ass didn't hear my voice—I grabbed the shifter by his arm and yanked him along with me down the hallway to my room. He tried to shrug me off, and he was surprisingly strong, but I was stronger. One of the many reasons the Council had kept me alive and on their side.

Reaching my room, I pushed the door open, shoving him inside and slamming it closed. He whirled around and we both froze staring at each other with lips parted and eyes wide in surprise. In his case it was my hair that made him to pause, I had no doubt. For me on the other hand …

There was something about him. He wasn't perfect by any stretch, with his square jaw covered in stubble and his nose slightly crooked from being broken one too many times. His cheekbones were high, and the color of his skin had a reddish hue that looked just right on him. It was his eyes that startled me the most. They were bright green like mine, only a golden ring pulsed around his irises, while the pupil kept flicking from round to vertical. Cat eyes.

The pounding of feet in the hallway was enough for me to snap out of my daze.

It was enough for him, too.

Hatred burned so intently on his face that it buckled my knees. We had no time left for a brawl, so I rushed to the window and threw it wide open while flipping my hand for him to hurry.

"Get out." My voice was raw from the smoke I'd inhaled earlier.

Instead of leaving, he was in front of me in a second. I couldn't breathe. His thick fingers wrapped around my neck and he squeezed for all he was worth. My lungs started burning and the pounding of feet was getting closer.

"Killing me is not worth you dying here tonight," I rasped, and his eyebrows hit his hairline. A brown lock of hair fell over his forehead and covered one of his eyes. "Go."

I watched the war in his strange eye until dark spots started dancing at the edges of my vision. Then I gulped air when he realized I wasn't fighting back because he released me. Choking for breath, I watched him crawl out of the window.

"Brooklyn." My croak made him turn, and confusion clouded his features. "My name."

"I will kill you next time I see you, Brooklyn," he spat, his deep voice sending ghostly fingers crawling over my body. I shivered.

"I can't wait." I told the empty window just as the door opened behind me.

I had no time to even ask what she was doing here before Veronica snatched the silk I was still clutching in one fist as she pushed me at the door with a hiss. "Keep your mouth shut, Bee." The same door that opened again just as

I was about to crash into it, but I was pushed to the wall as it pressed hard against my chest.

"What do you want Johnathan?" Veronica's voice was calm and clear like she didn't just rush into my room like a female possessed.

"You?" Johnathan barked infuriated. "Where is Brooklyn?"

"How should I know? Have you seen the smoke out there? It's so thick you have to cut your way through it."

"Where is he?" the kiss ass snarled, and I held my breath wondering what my friend thought she was doing.

"Who? You have imaginary friends now, darling?" Sugar oozed out of her mouth, and that only made him roar at her in rage. Veronica's gasp was a dagger in my chest.

Before I could push out from behind the door, he snatched her and was gone, which left me standing in the middle of my room with dread pooling in the pit of my stomach.

What had I done …

Chapter Six

Two days.

For two days they wouldn't tell me anything. All my questions fell on deaf ears. I wasn't allowed to leave my room, and the second I tried opening the door one of the goons would slam it shut in my face. Four of them were positioned in the hallway, which made me a prisoner. It was the same shit I'd gone through in the cages, only no one came to forcefully take my blood and it looked nice. Normal.

Which made it worse.

All the banging of my fists on the door until it cracked were ignored. My throat was raw from screaming and threatening them, but it was like no sound penetrated past the four walls, and the window was now barred. I had no idea what was happening to Veronica and that was what was slowly making me crazy. I hoped with everything in me that she was okay.

I hoped so badly it was driving me insane.

"What made you take the blame?" I whispered to the

empty room as my back slid slowly down the door and my ass hit the floor. "Why, Veronica? Why …"

My stomach caved in from hunger and my fangs were throbbing in my gums. It reminded me of the time I was locked up with no blood to quench my thirst for years, the feral state I was in when I clawed my way out of the cages. Veronica had found me. I'd been skin and bones, all curled up while shaking in the corner of a basement. Her kind face while she fed me her own blood and washed years-old dirt and dried blood off me came to my mind, and then I remembered all the whispered assurances that everything would be okay. Well, nothing was okay. Not when I was locked up and they were doing who knew what to her. Rage and hunger made me irrational, and I felt sanity slipping from my grasp. Pushing off the floor, I faced the door with every intention of kicking it out. My foot lifted off the ground.

The door clicked, swinging open on silent hinges.

Johnathan's arrogant face with his eyebrow arched in question at my crane pose in the middle of the room was the first thing I saw. "Well, that's a new one." His mumbled words annoyed the crap out of me.

"Get out of my way." I glared, tensing up to fight my way out.

"Your presence is needed. The Council wants to see you." Stepping to the side, he kept the stupid look of victory I never wanted to see on his face.

"Good, 'cause I want to see them, too." Walking by him without punching him was the hardest thing I'd ever done, but somehow I managed.

What I didn't manage was hiding my reaction to what met me when I walked out of the room. The walls were lined with bare-chested fighters, daggers and swords strapped to their bodies glinting in the lighting. Stern faces carved out of granite stared straight ahead, and not one of them blinked when I passed between them. Johnathan's presence at my back was an added bonus for my anxiety to hit new highs.

"They should've done this the moment I walked out of the cages," I said, and I wasn't speaking to anyone in particular. I was only trying to hide the fear choking me.

"What do you mean?" It took him a long time to speak. I supposed hearing me speak of the cages had caught him off guard.

"Have all the guards line my path wherever I go like the royalty I am." Glancing over my shoulder, I was confused by the widening of his eyes, but he recovered too fast for me to decipher the look. "It should be like this all the time. And you should bow when you address me, too."

"Keep talking shit like that and you won't last long enough to enjoy the guards." The kiss ass even went as far as shoving me between his shoulder blades, which made me stumble forward.

Good thing too or I would've missed the unassuming people sprinkled between all the massive bodies. My blood turned to ice when I saw their lips moving in a chant and their hands gliding in front of them.

Witches.

The damn Council brought the witches into their nest. That would explain why I couldn't break out of my room, as well as why no one got pissed enough at my screaming to come and shut me up. The only place I'd seen the witches was when metal bars were surrounding me, their chants keeping be compliant and turning my brain into goo. How did shit get this bad, and especially without any warning whatsoever? So lost in my panic, I didn't realize I'd reached the chamber of the Council until Johnathan yanked me next to him with a firm grip on my arm. I didn't break that arm only because I was still trying to process what I just saw throughout the mansion. Fucking witches were sitting among us. They were so rare to find that if I told anyone they guarded the cages they'd think I was hallucinating because I'd been deprived of nourishment. How the fuck did the Council find so many of them? And how did they have the guts to flaunt them in our faces? I counted at least fifteen from my room to the chamber.

"Go in," the guard that entered the chamber grumbled as he came out.

It was the second time I'd come face to face with the Council and only someone's grip on my arm kept me standing. Seeing Veronica bloodied on her knees in the middle of the wide room cracked open my heart and my legs almost gave out. Her bruised face shook sharply in a no, which was the only thing that stopped me from bolting to her. My gaze snapped at the three males who were watching me intently with various expressions plastered all over their faces. The leering disgust and anger I could deal with. It was the antic-ipation in Isaiah's eyes that sent ice shards through my center.

"Brooklyn, I am pleased to see you are unharmed." Frederic's gaze flicked to my neck where the purple and blue fingerprints of the shifter's hand had long since disappeared.

"I'm sure you are." It was out before I could stop myself. "Sire," I added lamely through my teeth.

"Come closer, child." Samir beckoned me with his hand, and Johnathan finally released the death grip he had on my arm, leaving red lines where his fingers used to be.

"You see, Brooklyn. Veronica here was not who we

50

thought she was." Isiah spoke as my numb legs carried me to stand next to Samir. I curled my fingers around the seams of my pants to stop my hands from shaking. "She was in cahoots with our enemies and helping them plan an attack while we took care of her as one of our own."

"She is one of us," I snapped at him.

"Bee, don't." Veronica's cracked voice was barely above a whisper, and that sound stabbed me right in the chest.

"Is she now?" Turning his upper body to better face me, Isaiah arched an eyebrow while he eyed me like a cat would a cornered mouse.

"She is loyal to the Syndicate. I would place my life as an assurance." Ignoring Veronica's burning stare, I kept my focus on Isaiah.

"Yet she helped the shifter who attacked our home escape." Cocking his head to the side, he smoothed the fabric of his robes unhurriedly. "What say you of that, Brooklyn? Will you still place your life on the line on her behalf?"

"He must've forced her." Blurting out the first thing that came to mind, I lifted my chin stubbornly. I had every intention on fighting them tooth and nail to let her go.

"Forced her?" Barking out a laugh, he exchanged looks with Frederic and Samir and dread started pressing on my shoulders like a boulder. "The one that managed to kill sixty-three of our kind decided to force our little Veronica here to help him escape? He sure could've picked someone smarter for that. No offense dear." Isaiah threw the last part at Veronica and my jaw almost hit the floor.

"I'm sure he didn't have time to do IQ tests." Samir snorted at my snarl.

"If he picked her for his escape, perhaps she had help

from someone smarter." Muttering under his breath, Frederic didn't lift his head from polishing his nails on his robes.

"I'd ask if it was Johnathan, but you said smart, so ..." My pursed lips were just to spite the kiss ass. Veronica's soft snort had tears burning the back of my eyes.

"The things you say, child." Chuckling, Samir stretched out on his chair and shook his head. "Always so entertaining."

Johnathan snarled and glared, obviously disagreeing with him.

"Did you help your friend?" Isaiah finally cut to the chase, and I had every intention of taking the blame. It was me who did it, after all. My mouth opened—

"Brooklyn had nothing to do with it. I did it all on my own." There was no trace of the broken female I'd found on her knees in the room when Veronica's voice sliced the air. "I helped the shifter, and she didn't know anything about it."

"And she finally confessed." Very slowly, Isaiah turned to my friend with a look of triumph. "You see, Veronica here denied everything no matter how hard we tried to convince her otherwise."

I was so aware of their methods of convincing that I was ready to puke all over them.

"I'm still unsure it was all her ..." Isaiah cut off with a look of horror and betrayal I'd never seen on his face before when my friend got to her feet, grabbed the pendant hanging around her neck, and ripped it off.

My heart stopped as I watched it dangle from her fist.

"Fuck you," she spat at the Council as she threw the pendant at Isaiah's head, nailing him in the middle of the forehead.

It all happened so fast.

All three Council members jumped to their feet, and I flinched away from them. Frederic and Samir roared insults at Veronica, while she stood proudly facing them with a serene smile on her face. Isiah materialized next to her as the guards burst through the doors from all the shouting, daggers clutched in their hands. Veronica's gaze didn't leave mine as she mouthed *"Love you, Bee."*

And those was her last words spoken. Striking like the viper he was, Isaiah sunk his fangs into her neck and ripped out her throat with a firm shake of his head. Blood sprayed in a wide arch until his face was bathed in it, and Veronica's lashes fluttered before hiding her warm, brown eyes from me forever. I stood there numb and horrified, my feet glued to the floor while my mind shrieked so loud it drowned out all the other noise around me.

Something inside me broke.

A chasm opened in my chest, and it swallowed everything I was so I no longer existed. My legs gave out and I dropped on the floor, my body shaking so bad I could hear my teeth chattering. I didn't see him rip her heart out, that would've killed me right there and then. Horror from what I witnessed, fear of what was next, and most of all soul-wrenching guilt pulled me under like a crashing wave. I couldn't breathe. Someone was screaming. It was so broken and loud. A window shattered to the side, the glass falling like rain over the tiles and making chiming noises as if it was music to accompany the mournful cry. A sharp pain in my throat as my vocal cords ripped told me it was me screaming.

Everything seemed surreal.

So when the sound of fighting echoed above me, I didn't think anything of it. Nor did I blink an eye when my curled-up form was lifted off the floor and I was wrapped in two strong arms that for some stupid reason made me feel safe instead of afraid for my life. I think I heard Samir's voice say *"Get her out of here,"* but that couldn't be the truth.

Roars and things breaking sounded one moment, and the next cold air hit me like a blast that made me shake harder in the cradle of the arms holding me. Whoever it was that snatched me was running, and the way his feet pounded the ground and jostled my body lulled me into a numbing sleep. The last thing I saw was a set of electric green eyes looking down at my face, but I could've sworn the pupils were vertical. That was okay though, because I was no longer alive.

I was dead.

I died in that chamber with Veronica, and all of this was just a dream.

Chapter Seven

Drifting in and out of consciousness was like a drowning man coming up for air just to be yanked under again until his lungs burned for oxygen, though nothing he did would help his predicament. Soft sounds were penetrating my mind, coming and going until they blended together, leaving only a constant buzzing in my ears that drove me insane. Everything was blurry when my eyelashes managed to unglue themselves from my cheekbones, but the light would burn my eyes until hot tears trickled down my face and soaked into my ears and neck.

I couldn't care less about any of it.

I just wanted to sleep and never wake up.

I had no idea how long this went on before a loud boom like a meteor crashing through the roof of a house made me jolt out of blissful darkness and bolt out of the bed I was sleeping on. No, not a bed. A couch that had seen better days, with a few springs poking out of the faded fabric. My head jerked left and right as I crouched next to it, my body ready to spring into action at any moment. Another crash from somewhere on my right sounded, but it was a lot less loud than what originally woke me up. Craning my neck, I dared to peek over the back of the stupid couch with my heart thrumming in my throat.

"It was about time you woke up." The deep voice made me shiver, and it took me a second to place it. "I was debating if I should just bury you alive."

I stood there staring openmouthed at the shifter until a kink developed in my neck. My head felt funny and I couldn't remember how the hell I got here in this dump with the one person who'd promised to kill me the next time we crossed paths. Lifting up from my crouch, I took a cautious step back, but he didn't notice. Still with his back to me, he kept banging shit on the table in the tiny kitchen, which was made smaller by his imposing presence in the middle of it. Every time he threw whatever he found in the bag he was holding on the tabletop, it felt like someone was pounding a nail in the middle of my forehead.

"Would you stop that?" On the fifth bang, I had to groan out the plea.

"Did I disturb your beauty sleep, your highness?" He sneered, spinning around to face me.

His intriguing face left me mute for a moment, just enough to admire the raw masculinity wafting off his chiseled body in waves. Not even his twisted-in-hatred face took away from his animalistic appeal to me. Or I could've had a concussion because someone hit me across the head. That was a bigger possibility, because I couldn't be so dumb that I'd ogle a shifter while being enclosed in a place with him.

"No asshole, my head feels like it might explode from whatever you did to me to get me here." Snapping out of the idiocy, I snapped at him like it was his fault I'd been checking him out.

Well, it kind of was his fault. He could've eaten crappy food and given himself a beer belly. That would've helped right about now.

"The only thing I did was save your life." If he punched me, I would've had more air inflating my lungs. "That makes us even. I don't want to owe anything to any of your kind."

"Back track a bit there, buddy. Say what again?" While he was glaring at me, I used the opportunity to pinch myself hard on the thigh in case I was still dreaming. My mouth twisted in a grimace from the pain, which made the shifter eye me as if I would lose my shit at any moment.

"You really don't remember what happened?" Searching my eyes, he leaned back on the table and crossed his tree-trunk arms across his chest.

"Remember what exactly?" spelling it out slowly for him, I wondered if maybe he was a little special.

The last thing I remembered was helping him jump out of my window. Did he jump after he threatened me, or did he change his mind about waiting to kill me, hit me on the head, and drag me here with him? That would explain everything. It would've served me right if that was the case, too.

"Your Council," he said Council like it was the vilest thing touching his tongue, "performed an execution in their chamber while you watched." The back of my head started throbbing before numbness spread over my skull and shoulders, but he kept talking. "After ripping the blonde's throat out, one of them was coming straight for you with his fangs bared when I used the distraction their guards created to get you out of there."

I could tell he wasn't telling the truth, at least not all of it, but for some reason I found the idea of compelling him to tell me the whole truth repulsive. Everything came rushing back with crippling clarity. The chasm of loss opened in my chest again, and the guilt doubled me over until I dropped me to my knees. The dreary place blurred through the torrent of tears spilling from my eyes, and my throat felt so tight I couldn't even sob as loud as I wanted. Only tiny gasps were passing through my mouth, which was open in a silent scream. My body started shaking uncontrollably again and there was nothing I could do to pull myself together.

Warm, steady hands wrapped around my shoulders, the heat of the palms almost burning my chilled skin through the fabric of my sleeveless shirt. Blinking fast, I cleared my vision just enough to see the shifter's face and the worry clouding his green eyes. Sucking in a shuddering breath, I tried speaking but only one word came out.

"Veronica …"

He waited a long moment, but when nothing else came he spoke warily. "Was that the one who was executed?"

Unable to answer, I nodded jerkily as I fought to suck in a full breath.

"She was your family?" At that point, I wondered if he actually enjoyed this. Torture would've been preferred over talking about the one I'd lost. The sadness I saw in his gaze was the only thing that made me continue punishing myself.

"My best friend," I croaked. "The only family I had left."

"I'm sorry, Brooklyn." Hearing my name pass his lips pulled me out of the darkness that was dragging me into the never-ending abyss.

I acutely felt the loss of his warmth when one of his hands lifted off my shoulder, but my eyes fluttered closed when his fingers tangled in my hair and he smoothed it away from my face. My eyes snapped open when he cupped my cheek, the rough skin of his thumb wiping away the tears that kept rolling down my cheeks and soaking into the front of my shirt. My body leaned forward, the need to crash my lips to his and lose myself in the animalistic urge of lust so I could stop thinking about Veronica pushing me to do the stupidest thing ever. Still focused on my tearful gaze, he did the same, leaning forward until our faces were so close I could feel his warm breath on my lips. Then his eyes dropped to my neck where my pendant swayed with my movement and his hand jerked back as if I'd burned him, the movement so full of force he almost fell on his ass.

"You need to feed," he spat in disgust while jumping to his feet and avoiding my startled gaze.

"I'm good, but thank you for caring." My emotionless tone made him pause in his dash for the kitchen. "And thank you for saving me." The tone of my voice told him I hated that he did it. "Why did you attack the Syndicate?" I spoke to his back. "What was that smoke you used to turn them aggressively at each other?" nothing came forward, so I continued. " Who was it that made you save my life? You won't answer any of my questions, will you?"

The shifter didn't answer, nor did he turn to look at me. He disappeared, returning to the small living room with a brown rabbit wiggling in his large hand. I stared at it blankly for long enough that he actually shoved it under my nose, which only made me flinch away from it.

"Take it." He waved the poor creature in my face. "It isn't much, but it'll be enough until you can go find something on your own. I'd like to sleep with both eyes closed tonight instead of worrying that you might want a snack."

"You can't be serious." Slapping his hand away when he brought the writhing creature in front my face again, I scowled at him. "I can control my urges just fine, I assure you. Starving or not, the last place I'd want to satisfy my hunger would be your throat."

He didn't look convinced, so my glare deepened.

"Move the damn thing out of my face." He tensed when I bared my fangs, but I had to give him credit for not pouncing to attack me thanks to my aggressive display.

"We will do it your way." Frowning at the rabbit in his hand, he shrugged his wide shoulders. "But the moment I feel your eyes on my pulse, I'll end you. Am I clear?"

"You have no idea," I drawled, the whole rabbit thing paired with his show of compassion bringing some sort of control to my turbulent emotions.

I was still numb from losing Veronica, and the guilt would be my companion for a very long time, but I decided in that moment that locking up the crippling pain would serve me best. There would be plenty of time to grieve for my friend. I owed her something more than crying over the loss of her life. I owed her revenge. Until tonight, all I'd wanted was to screw the Syndicate in ways that they'd never guess until it was too late. Now I had better motivation.

The Council would pay for her death with their lives.

After I took everything they cared for from them.

Pushing up on my feet, I blew out a breath and straightened my clothing, rubbing at my eyes with the backs of my hands. I would not dishonor my friend by moping around like some fool. She would be disappointed at how pathetic and weak I was if I dealt with the situation that way. Good thing my little rebellions left me with a lot of favors to collect. Ignoring the wary way the shifter was watching me, I headed right for the door.

"Where do you think you are going?" he growled at my

back, dropping the poor creature on the floor. I watched it bolt under the sofa.

"To visit a friend." Turning away and yanking the door open, I didn't close it because he was already breathing down my neck. "I guess you'll be coming along then."

"Until I decide what to do with you, I'm not letting you out of my sight."

My body shook a little and I shivered from the barely contained promise of violence in his deep voice. Unable to help myself, I looked at him over my shoulder. The intensity in his green gaze took my breath away.

"Lead the way, Brooklyn," he snarled, and my shoulders lifted all the way to my ears from the deep sigh rushing past my lips.

"It's going to be a long night," I murmured, and then I led the way, doing exactly as he asked.

Hopefully Alice had some catnip at her place. Otherwise, I might've just throttled the shifter before I killed him.

Chapter Eight

It should've been weird to have my back turned while a shifter was prowling right behind me, but the one keeping me in his sights at all times somehow put me at ease. It could be the fact that he did get me out when I was surely going to die, but I had a nagging feeling it was more than that. There was just something about him. I couldn't even get myself to use my voice to get him off my ass. Maybe it was the way he bravely walked inside the mansion full of Atua when most of us that lived there wanted to do nothing but get the hell out. Or the way he actually looked insulted when I got him out of Johnathan's way and made him run.

Whatever it was, I had every intention of figuring it out.

He intrigued me.

"Where are we going?" This was the third time he'd asked the same.

He also annoyed me a little, too.

On the second trip around the same block, I could practically hear the cogs in his mind churning with everything he was fighting not to say. There was not a force in this world that could've kept the small smile off my face. The poor guy was brimming so much with unasked questions that the air around him felt charged. Light mist started sprinkling from the sky, which did nothing to help my unlikely companion. Apparently, what they said was true and cats and water didn't mix well. I, on the other hand, did not mind it, or the sharp bite in the air nipping at my skin. I had too many emotions still waiting to erupt like a volcano at any moment, so the cold kind of helped keep my mind off of them.

"Why are we walking around the same block again?" He couldn't keep his question to himself anymore.

"I thought shifters liked being taken out for a walk around the block." Keeping him at my back so he didn't see the grin I was fighting, I shrugged a shoulder and made sure my tone was conversational. "Should I have leashed you to make it more appealing to you?"

My back hit the wall of the building hard enough for the structure to tremble for a second, and my teeth rattled from the force of the hit. My heartbeat sped up when he pressed his body to mine and pinned me between brick and a wall of muscle. I kept my gaze steady on his eyes, which were turned into slits and spitting venom.

"Do not play games with me, female." The threat was unmistakable in the words that were spoken softly over my lips. The hand around my throat tightened, not cutting off my air completely but enough to make me fight for a breath.

"Let me guess. Or you'll kill me," I deadpanned.

"Do you wish to die?"

"No, but I do wish you could keep your mouth shut." And just because I thought his arrogance needed a little wakeup call, I had us in a reverse position before he could see it coming, and this time it was his back hitting the wall. I didn't have a hand around his neck. The tips of my fangs made dents on his throat, and I knew he barely felt it, but it was enough to pierce his skin. "Not knowing who you are attacking can cost you your life, kitty."

His body shivered and goosebumps erupted on the skin where my breath puffed up with each word. I could feel his heart kicking into a faster rhythm, and the barely audible growl deep in his chest did not escape me. His jaw clenched and a muscle jumped in it when he realized his body's reaction. It must've chipped at his pride, no doubt. I actually knew it did because he was fighting not to shift.

"Either bite or back off." His voice was rough, the rasp in it doing stupid things to my girly parts, so I pushed away from him.

"I just want to make sure no one is following us," I answered his question from a while ago after we stared at each other for way too long, our fast breaths curling like smoke from our mouths and nostrils in the cold night. "You can think of me anything you want, but I'm not trying to get my friends killed." Unable to understand the slight frown between his eyebrows or the confusion blanketing his face, I didn't even try.

Spinning on my heel, I started down the sidewalk again, grateful that this part of town was mostly abandoned and empty. Pages of old newspapers were dancing in the breeze curling and flopping like dying butterflies in the cast of the yellow streetlights. A few wrecked cars were parked on the side of the road, their wheels missing and bricks propped under them to hold their weight. Broken widows stared at us like gaping holes and doors leaned tipped to the side after being ripped off their hinges. Faint light met my gaze from time to time from a depleted tiny home with peeled-off paint and drying grass in the front yard. The stench of urine and who knew what else was soaked into the asphalt, and no amount rain or washing would ever take it off. It suited me just fine for what I was doing, but I never understood why Alice lived here.

For that reason, I never asked.

The shifter stayed silent and deep in thought until we reached the rectangular gray building with a flat roof and boarded double doors. The glass was smashed a long time ago, Alice told me, but plywood apparently did wonders to keep the place safe. It didn't look safe at all to me, but I never understood humans in general. She might be right. Pushing the gate of the thigh-high wooden fence I was across the small pathway and up the two steps in no time, the shifter right behind me. My hard rap on the door made the plywood rattle, so I yanked my hand back not wanting to break it.

Silence met me, apart from the few barks and the screech of a bird.

The shifter shuffled his feet impatiently behind me, but I stayed staring at the doors willing them to open. Veronica's bruised and bloody face floated to the front of my mind as she mouthed *"I love you, Bee,"* and dread spread through me like a wave. My whole body tingled and cold sweat trickled down my spine. *Come on, Alice. Open the door,* I chanted in my head, but I was too afraid to open it myself because I was terrified of what I might find inside. I made sure no one followed us when I accompanied her here. There was no way anyone in the Syndicate knew where she was.

"We can go from the back." The shifter made me jump when he spoke from the side of the building. I didn't even hear him move.

"You don't have to kill me, kitty. You can just scare me

to death." I glared, and then was left with my mouth hanging open when he smiled.

It brightened his entire face. Straight white teeth blinked in the light of the streetlamp in the corner, stretching his full lips up his cheeks. His eyes lifted at the corners and humor made them brighter somehow. The harsh lines of his face softened, which gave him a boyish appeal and also shaved away the sternness I was used to seeing there.

"Little jumpy, are we?" Chuckling, he kept grinning and I couldn't help but join him.

At least he wasn't glaring at me.

That was a plus.

"You could say that twice." Jumping down over both steps, I joined him. "She might be at the back and didn't hear the knock, so you are right."

"One of your kind lives here?"

I couldn't blame him for sounding shocked. Atua loved their luxuries, and the more extravagant it was the better was their view on things. The Syndicate was more vain than the rest of us and flaunted their wealth for everyone to see. None of my kind would be found dead in a place like this.

"No, she's human."

The shifter made a strangled sound, so I whirled around with my knees bent and fangs bared because I thought he'd been hit. My head whipped left and right while he hacked, my gaze darting up and down the street to look for the attacker. Fury burned in my chest for not being more alert, and now there'd be a bloodbath in the middle of a human suburb. Abandoned or not, it was bound to get attention from the humans if the streets were painted red. And the Syndicate, for that matter.

"Where are you hurt?" Stepping around him, I covered

his body with mine as he pounded on his chest with a fist. "Speak, kitty. Where are you hurt?"

"Not hurt," he wheezed.

I slowly turned to face him. "Then what are you doing? Hacking out a hairball?" Frustrated that he freaked me out, I was frowning so hard a headache developed at the center of my forehead. I kept the street visible from the corner of my eye just in case.

"Stop calling me kitty," he croaked, and then then cleared his throat, a few more coughs following. "You are friends with a human?"

There'd been many times in my long life that I'd been given strange looks, mostly for the color of my hair and eyes, and occasionally for the word vomit coming out of my mouth before I had a chance to think better of it. Yet no one had looked at me like the shifter was at that moment. The expression on his face said that there was something not right with me. Like he was debating my existence as a being.

I didn't like it at all.

"So?" Jamming both fists on my hips, I scowled at him. "If that's a problem for you, get the fuck out of here. Go wait on the street."

"Not a problem at all," the shifter muttered, some emotion I couldn't name flashing in his eyes. "I was just surprised, that's all."

He was still watching me strangely, and that made me uncomfortable, so I left him there and moved quickly around the building. It was as if I was trying to escape his scrutiny, or maybe the way he made me feel while his eyes were on me. I didn't know which, though. When he caught up with me, I thought I heard him murmur, *"I'm either dreaming or this is a different dimension."* But something fell inside Alice's home with a loud bang and I ignored his outburst.

"Speed up, kitty."

"Dominic."

"What?" Stopping at the corner of the building, I glanced back at him.

"My name is Dominic. Stop calling me kitty. It's annoying."

"Aww, look at you all friendly and stuff." Grinning like a fool at the grumble in his chest, I even winked at him. "Now stay here so you don't freak her out. She's little ... peculiar, you could say."

"She's human," he said it slowly like I had no idea what species that was.

"And your point is what? She's dumb and has no survival instinct? Have you seen yourself in the mirror lately?"

His eyebrows hit his hairline and his jaw fell slightly open while he looked me up and down. "If I ... I have seen ... in the mirror ..." he sputtered, but I waved him off and rounded the corner.

He could spend his time waiting around and trying to put a full sentence together. I had to see Alice to assure myself that she was still alive. I'd deal with everything else later. A tall metal fence blocked my way to the back door, the closed-up area littered with dog toys, obstacles for train-ing, and a few cages that made bile rise in my throat. I'd have to get rid of those later when I was done here because no being deserved to be caged. Alice never struck me as the cruel type, but how well did I actually know her? The human and I would have some words when I saw her. And I would see her, because if she was gone, I might just lose my shit.

Curling my fingers through the metal links, I climbed the fence fast, vaulting my body over it and dropping on the other side in a crouch. Avoiding looking at the cages, I rushed to the back door and reached for the handle when I heard the metal of the fence rattle gently. My head snapped back in time to see Dominic drop on the balls of his feet. Straightening, he cocked an eyebrow in a dare for me to say something as he strutted across the yard.

"Which part of wait didn't you understand?" I hissed under my breath.

"The waiting part." The asshole grinned and arrogance oozed off him in spades. "I don't trust you, so you are not leaving my sight."

Clenching my jaw so hard my face hurt, I ignored his jab and yanked the back door open a lot harder than was needed. The hinges cracked, then there was a tinkling like chimes over the small wooden porch where I stood. Left with the door in my hand, I closed my eyes praying for patience, especially when I heard him snort at my back. Flipping around, I shoved the door at his chest, which made him stumble back while trying to take hold of it.

"Stay." Whisper-yelling the command, I entered the building because I was unwilling to deal with his arrogant ass, but also well aware he would not listen.

A dark mudroom with a few pairs of shoes kicked all over the floor and jackets hanging on a hook on the wall met me, while another closed door half made out of glass was blocking the inside of the house. By the time I took hold of it to open it, Dominic was at my back, the heat of his body reminding me that the shifter was becoming a pain in the ass. A lot slower I opened the second door and stepped inside a white open room, which was bright from the dozen floor lamps shining all around it. Sheer white curtails were pinned on the windowless walls as decoration.

It had barely any furniture, just a small couch covered in animal hairs and a coffee table in front of it, but that was why the rest of the floor was overwhelmed with large colorful pillows. It felt like we just walked in through a time gate and found ourselves back in the eras of Sultans and Emperors. All sorts of crystals, rocks, and dreamcatchers littered the walls, and I finally found the human standing in the middle of it, blinking owlishly at us through her round glasses. She looked like a child caught with her hand in the cookie jar, her lips slightly parted and her hands fisting in her moss-colored flowing dress.

"What the *fuck* is going on here?" Dominic's snarl made me squeeze my eyes shut in a groan.

"Oh, Alice." The words were just a deep sigh.

Chapter Nine

If you had never seen a wolf smirking at you, I wasn't sure I had the adequate words to describe it. Plus, I had a feeling nobody would believe me anyways. The shifter's tail was flicking lazily behind him and his upper lip very slowly curled at the corners. To add salt to injury, he plopped his stupid ass on one pillow and tilted his muzzle to the side as if daring me to call him out on it.

The feline shifter at my back released a low, terrifying sound from deep in his chest that made all the short hairs on my body rise to attention.

The human didn't notice anything.

"Brooklyn, umm … hey, hi. How nice you came over," Alice stuttered, her eyes darting left and right as if looking for an escape. Her cheeks turned bright red, and I frowned as my body tensed. She looked ready to hyperventilate. "It's not what you think!" A finger stabbed the air toward me. "Well, it is, actually but I can totally explain. You see, I tried, but he won't get in the car so I can drop him off. So … basically, it's not my fault. Right? Right!"

"Did she just answer her own question?" Dominic grumbled from behind me, but I kept my face expressionless and continued to stare at Alice. Anger burned a hole in my gut. The human was going to get all of us killed.

The shifter from the plane, who was supposed to be in one of the reservations for a while now, pinned his ears to his skull and bared his long, sharp teeth at me. The wolf stood, and he shifted through the pillows to get closer to the human before he nudged her behind him as if trying to protect her from me. The bigger shock was Alice's hand sinking into his fur, her fingers twisting in it to keep her balance when she stumbled. My cocked eyebrow snapped the human from her flabbergasted state, and I held my breath waiting for the disaster to happen. At that point, I wasn't sure if I wanted to scream or laugh at the situation.

At least she was alive. There was that.

"Actually, Brooklyn," Her chin jutted out, and in her right mind she glared at me. "What the hell are you doing here, huh? Didn't you say we had to stay away from each other because of that dead woman you found two days ago?" As soon as the words were out, she gasped and slapped a hand over her mouth, her eyes almost popping out of her sockets when they locked on Dominic behind me, who was muttering curses under his breath throughout the entire debacle. I thought I also heard him say, "This can't be fucking happening."

I agreed.

"I misspoke." Alice hurried to assure him, waving her arms like a traffic controller. "It wasn't Brooklyn who found a dead person at all. At all! As a matter of fact, it was a dream I had that I was telling her about, and we decided it was a sign to take a break from hanging out. Right Brooklyn? Remember how we laughed about it? Yeah, just a dream, that's all." Inhaling loudly and sounding like a whale when she ran out of air, she laughed a little hysterically. "A dream ... yeah ... I have those sometimes ..." The last part was murmured, and her frown was worrisome.

Daring to take a chance, I looked over my shoulder at Dominic to see if he would attack first and ask questions later, but my stomach dropped to my feet instead. It was worse than I thought, and honestly, he was probably thinking both of us had a screw loose. He had his eyes squeezed shut as he pinched the bridge of his nose between a thumb and a forefinger. Nothing could've prepared me for this fiasco, so I decided to ignore the whole thing, starting from the moment I stepped foot in this damn place. Side-stepping pillows and kicking them to the side, I made a path to the small couch and sat on it, which gave me the perfect view of everyone in the room.

"Let's try this again, shall we?" Alice shrunk back when I spoke, her shoulders curling in as if she was hurting. Dominic's intent gaze made me feel like I was standing two feet from the sun and my skin was about to melt off my bones. "Why is he still here, Alice? You know very well that both of us can get in a lot of trouble if they find him."

"I'm not afraid of going to jail," she barked stubbornly, shocking Dominic enough that his jaw dropped to his chest.

"If they find him, neither you nor I will be going to jail. We will die. I explained this to you." Praying for patience, I tried to reason with her.

For all her faults, I actually liked Alice. She was kind and compassionate. Something I didn't see often apart from ... Pushing the thoughts of Veronica aside, I focused on the human. It was safer that way.

"How will they know, Brooklyn? He is not microchipped. I know because I checked. There is no way anyone can claim he is theirs," she continued, arguing her point but not aware of the glares both shifters gave her when she mentioned the microchip.

"He is not a pet, Alice."

"Oh, yeah?" Glee spread across her face. "Watch this, Miss now it all." Pushing the glasses that had slid down her nose up, she even cleared her throat. "Sit," she snapped at the shifter and pointed at her feet. It was my turn to smirk, despite the situation.

I raised my eyebrow at the snarling wolf.

"No, bad boy. No growling, you hear me. Sit!" Color me surprised, but the asshole actually walked up to her and sat down, although his upper lip was curled over sharp canines.

"I can't watch this it's too painful to see his humilia-tion." Dominic's were loud and furious. "What sort of insanity is this? Is this what the Council does with those who go missing? You turn them into human pets? What the fuck have you done to him?"

"Human pets?" Alice snorted. "As opposed to alien pets? You sound like my dad." she muttered, but I ignored her and kept my eyes on Dominic to see if he would lose his battle for control and shift in her living room. Or whatever this room was called.

"Do you know what your friend Brooklyn is, human?" The word "human" was snarled like a curse as he took a threatening step toward her.

Shifters were loyal and very protective when it came to their own. But outside of that, they hated the Atua and didn't think much of the humans at all. He might think twice before attacking someone that would give him a fair fight, although from what I knew about him, that was debatable to say the least. He wouldn't blink an eye to pounce on the weak species scowling at him. But leave it to Alice to make things worse.

"Yeah I do. Brooklyn stands up for those that have no voice to stand up for themselves." I groaned, and Dominic's eyebrows crawled all the way to his hairline. "She saves these poor animals so they are not put down," Alice told him proudly, but it only made me wish I could turn invisible.

"She saves them?" But Alice was not finished talking over him.

"That makes her a badass in my book, and I couldn't give a rat's ass about anything else she might be. I don't see you bringing any around, now do I?" And to light a match to the fire, she didn't stop at that. "Which makes you, Sir, ignorant, or a coward."

I was in front of Dominic with a hand pressed at the center of his chest before she finished the last word. His eyes flickered to his vertical pupils and back and his face contorted in rage, but luckily no fur sprouted over it. Well, not much anyway. It took most of my strength to hold him in place without fighting him in front of Alice.

"How did you do that?" she gasped from behind me, her words cracking as the wolf shifter growled a warning at Dominic.

"I came here for a reason, Dominic." Keeping my voice steady, I waited until his gaze locked on mine. "I need her help, and she can't do that if she has a heart attack or if you hurt her."

This part was tricky, and I was sure Alice wondered why we were just staring at each other, but I hoped she was startled enough from my speed that she wouldn't think much of it. Keeping my tone low so only he could hear me, a feather tickled the back of my throat when his eyes dropped to my lips so he could also read the words I was saying.

"It won't be long before the Council orders a hunt for you and me, so we don't have much time. I have no intention of going down without taking as many of them with me as I can. Do you? Fair enough you don't want to share information about what you are up to, but as much as we dislike each other we can at least work together on a common goal." He lifted his gaze and searched mine for a moment before cautiously moving his head to indicate that he was on the same page. Distrust still lurked in the depths of his green irises, but I knew that was as good as I'd get from him.

I released the pressure on the hand I used to hold him back, and he leaned into my palm when I tried to remove it. My own heart kicked up, the beat matching the drumming of his under my skin. The scent that was uniquely him filled my nostrils and clouded my head. I wet my dry lips to moisten them. His eyes zeroed in on the move, the predatory glint making goosebumps erupt all over me. I was so focused on his smell and the way he felt under my hand that I missed everything else. That was until Alice spoke.

"Umm ... guys?" The timid way she said it made me whirl around, my body coiled up to attack. "Someone is trying to enter through the front door." A human whispering was like someone shouting to our ears. I was sure Alice meant well.

"Stay with her," I snapped at the wolf shifter, but I was already moving toward the front of the building with Dominic.

I saw the wolf herding Alice into the far corner, the human protesting and trying to shove him away the entire time, but still he placed himself like a living shield in front of her. The room we were in opened into a long hallway with a couple of doors on either side of it, sounds of dogs whining, cats hissing, and birds chirping coming from behind them. At the end, it curved into an entrance area half the size of the place we left Alice in, made into a small apartment with a dining table that had two chairs, a TV stand that had more candles than an actual TV, and a small kitchen to the right.

Judging by the smell, bundles of sage hung from all cabinet doors, masking the scent of whoever it was that was shuffling in front of the building. Their feet were silent, but the old wood of the narrow porch gave the person away. A soft cracking noise as if the floor was sighing from the weight crackled in my ears.

Dominic touched my upper arm to get my attention, pointing first at himself then at the kitchen. Offering just a jerk of my head as a nod, I didn't move my eyes from the closed front door. Tonight, Alice would learn that plywood was not safe by any stretch of the imagination. And that was when the unthinkable happened. My foot stepped on a dog toy, the squeak the damn thing released making me jump a foot of the floor. I froze, Dominic froze, and so did whoever was trying to break in. My body was so tense I thought I'd break if I twitched a muscle.

The door exploded inward.

Shrapnel made of plywood and leftover glass flew at me, the tiny cuts on my skin forgotten when a shadow fell over the threshold. Noah blocked the yellow light coming from the streetlamps behind him. His wide shoulders hid the glow, casting his face in darkness that made him look more sinister than he had any right to be. His deep eyes lit from within and pinned me in place as he bared his fangs at me. All my rage bubbled up to the surface when I faced him.

"Brooklyn, we meet again," he muttered and stepped inside.

"For the last time, asshole."

Noah pounced, his fist hitting me on the temple and snapping my neck painfully to the side. Lifting my foot, I kicked him with a flat foot in the stomach to create space between our bodies. He stumbled back but didn't move away much. Both his arms and legs turned into a blur, every hit bringing dark spots dancing in front of my eyes. My mind was screaming that it was impossible for him to be that strong. Electric green eyes came into my vision from behind Noah, but a crash coming from the back of the house made Dominic pull back into the shadows. Footsteps thundered down the hallway, Alice coming toward us with a shrill scream. Noah's head snapped that way.

My heart stopped. This was it. The end.

"Get out you fucker!" Screaming from the top of her lungs, Alice darted to join us, a floor lamp missing a shade clutched in her hands like a baseball bat. She swung it left and right in front of her, the long cord dangling from it slithering behind her like a snake. The crazy human must've broken the lamp so she could use it as a weapon. That was the crash that we heard. Alice skidded to a stop and her eyes widened in horror when Noah turned to meet her.

Throwing myself at the Atua, I tackled him on the floor just as the biggest black panther I'd ever seen jumped over us and blocked the way to Alice. Dominic's green eyes stared at me from the panther's face. He looked magnificent, all muscle and pure predatory power. Noah hissed at him, his fangs growing in size while he struggled under me.

Alice screamed again.

That was when it hit me. Noah wasn't that strong. I was holding back because I didn't want Alice to know what kind of monster she'd let in her home. Noah was here to kill me, and I stupidly fought him as if I was the human. My gums started throbbing and I felt my own fangs sliding down.

"Oh hell no ..." Alice's voice trailed off and disappeared down the hallway as she bolted back to where she came from, the cord of the lamp like a tail behind her.

"I will have so much fun with the human after I'm done with you." Noah groaned as he bucked under me. It grated on my nerves.

"Funny." The smile on my face removed his smirk. "It sounds to me like you expect to survive this."

I could've sworn the panther chuckled.

Chapter Ten

Sharp pain almost doubled me over when the Atua I had pinned to the floor slammed his fist to my side. I heard ribs cracking, my bones giving way under the hard impact. Teeth clenched and my core tensed as hard as a rock, I braced for more. Everything in me wanted to curl up in a ball so I could make myself as small of a target as I could, but that would've been signing my own death warrant. Noah had no intention on losing his advantage. The tides had turned, and he now had me on the floor looming over my smaller frame with fists hammering anywhere he saw an opening. All I had to do was open my mouth and things were going to change quickly. There was just one problem.

I didn't trust Dominic.

Not enough to play all my cards in the open. At this moment, however, while pain was blurring my thoughts and fear of what would happen to Alice, along with Veronica's death, weighing like a noose around my neck? I had no choice but to act first and remedy the situation later. Noah landed a few more punches while the realization hit me that the moment I allowed him to follow me to see Alice, I never had any intention of letting him live. Maybe I was not much better off than the Syndicate and the Council. Without Veronica to keep my sanity in check, the feral creature I was before, the one who escaped the cages, would rear its head and do anything to survive.

Even kill innocents.

I could taste my own blood in my mouth, but acid burned the back of my throat from those thoughts. My eyes squeezed shut by default when Dominic pounced at Noah's back, his paw the size of my head slashing the air with wicked, deadly claws. I might not have to kill the shifter if he killed me first. It was all about perspective, and if I didn't get my head out of my ass I was going to end up too weak from blood loss to protect Alice, let alone all my secrets.

Noah moved to the side to avoid the claws that tried to rake his back. My eyes locked on Dominic's and I stared unblinking at death for a split second that lasted too long for my sanity. His front leg jerked to the side and missed my neck by a mere inch before they sunk into the floor by my head. One of the sharp claws caught the chain holding my pendant around my throat, but it didn't break it. The momentum flung the panther forward, sending him sailing over me so close I felt the heat of his body warm my blanched face. He twisted in the air, the muscles under his shiny black fur bunching before he landed on his feet facing Noah again. Head lowered and ears pinned to the back of his head, the sound coming from deep in Dominic's chest was the most terrifying thing I'd heard in my life.

Goosebumps popped out over my arms and a shiver spread over my back and up my spine, but I took the moment for what it was: an opportunity to get rid of Noah. Scissoring my legs, I flipped my body over as well and landed in a crouch next to the panther. Every broken bone screamed in protest as they tried to mend, but I clenched my teeth and endured it silently. My balance suffered a little and I tipped to the side for just a second, which didn't go unnoticed by either male.

"I will skin your cat after I'm done with you." Noah sneered, pulling out a carved dagger from the back of his pants. Dust and animal hair covered him from head to toe, probably from rolling on the floor with me. It messed up his pristine appearance, for sure. Dominic's shoulders hunched much too close to the ground, so I knew he was about to attack.

"I wouldn't call him a cat, either. He gets edgy." Proud that I wasn't hissing the words because of my pain, I slowly stood and faced him, warily eyeing the dagger in his hand. "He might cough out a hairball at you."

Dominic paused because of my movement, and that gave me some time to think. There was something about the weapon that was sounding alarms in my head, but for the life of me I couldn't figure out why. I'd never seen anything like it before, but my skin crawled just thinking about it getting anywhere near me. Which was stupid if I looked at it rationally. For anyone to kill an Atua, they had to rip out our throat and take out our hearts. Noah couldn't kill me with the weapon alone. I knew that, I just doubted that fact because of the way its steel blinked at me as if trying to get my attention. Or warn me.

"You like it?" The corners of Noah's lips slowly tilted up when he noticed my gaze darting to the blade a few times. Twirling it in his hand, he took up a fighting stance and grinned menacingly. "It used to belong to your father."

What little blood I had left in my veins turned to ice. "He didn't get much of a chance to use it with his sentimentalities and dreams of living peacefully among those inferior to us. Luckily, I took it off his corpse before the rest arrived. It's spelled, you see. It doesn't miss its mark. Better suited for a warrior than a spineless maggot like him."

My mouth opened but no sound came out. I was so taken aback by his comment that I only realized he'd moved when blinding pain ripped a scream from my throat and warmth spread down my left side. My fingers came out red when I pressed my hand there, and Dominic shocked me by placing himself between Noah and me. I knew he wanted the Atua dead; he made no secret of it. Fighting alongside me was no surprise at all, either. Not if it helped remove one of us from the face of the earth. But to protect me? That I wasn't expecting, and it left me stunned while I stumbled back to lean on the wall.

"See? It always finds its mark." Gloating, Noah lifted the dagger to his mouth and licked my blood off the blade, closing his eyes blissfully.

Dominic pounced.

The panther collided with the Atua, his jaw clamping around the wrist holding the blade. Dominic's weight took both of them to the ground with a loud crash and a roar that came from Noah's mouth. The panther was shaking his head venomously while doing his best to remove Noah's hand from his arm, and I was unable to help him. Every time I tried to push off the wall it felt like my knees would give out. I knew what I had to do, but I still couldn't get myself to do it. Keeping it hidden for as long as I remembered, it felt like all the secrecy was for nothing if I gave myself away now.

The sky opened outside dumping a torrent of rain out

of nowhere. It splattered everywhere through the broken front doors, and the darkness lit up when lightning split the air and cast eerie shadows across the room. Thunder that rattled the windows and the foundation of the flimsy building followed. The panther and Noah were wrestling on the floor, the continuing lightning snapping across their features like the flash of a camera. Dominic was still chewing for all he was worth on the Atua's wrist. I took a deep breath, but a movement from the corner of my eye made my head turn in the direction of the hallway.

Alice's pale face poked from behind the wall, her wide eyes barely visible through the fogged-up glasses perched on her nose. Her mouth was open in horror and she clutched the wall in a white-knuckled grip like it was the only thing keeping her sane. I pushed off the wall and stumbled toward her, while her gaze flicked to me before doing a double take. I must've been a sight, all bruised and bloody with fangs sticking out from under my upper lip, because she screamed and bolted down the hallway again. What sounded like the human arguing with herself drifted from the back of the house a moment later, and holding onto the wall with one hand, I released a deep sigh. What a nightmare.

The males were now locked in twisted limbs, with Noah cuddling the panther by wrapping his legs around him. His free hand was jammed in Dominic's jaw as he tried to pry it open, but shockingly the Atua was still stubbornly clutching the dagger in his mangled hand. Squeezing my fist, I did what I'd never done before if there would be any witnesses left alive.

I spoke.

"Noah, stop." The tone of my voice changed into something sultry with a soft husk to it, the words rolling off my tongue with a subtle lilt that happened only when I used this gift, as Veronica liked to call it. "Release the dagger."

The Atua shook his head as if to clear it, but his body froze and the cluttering of the weapon on the floor chimed through the room. Dominic didn't waste time releasing the wrist from his jaw, and right after that he jumped on top of the dagger, kicking it behind him with a swat of his paw. Noah was still on his knees on the floor, a deep frown twisting his features while he fought the command. But I wasn't watching the Atua. I knew he wouldn't do anything I didn't allow him to do. My eyes were on the panther, who was looking at me like he had never seen me in his life.

It was not a common thing for Atua to be able to compel humans. Those that could were so few and far between that it was almost a myth that they boasted about. We were predators, after all, and that was just one more weapon in our arsenal that nature had given us. It was impossible to have that gift unless you were in the close circle of the Syndicate, in which case all bets were off and you could do whatever you wanted. Those who could were picked off quickly to join the Council, but they never survived very long. Cruelty was a virtue in the Syndicate. This new expression on the panther's face, more importantly his narrowed eyes, was because it was unheard of an Atua to compel one of our own. Or any supernatural for that matter.

Unless you were me, obviously.

Adrenaline made me shaky and my stomach was somersaulting like crazy while I held his gaze. The old fear of the cages clawed at my insides, and the room spun peculiarly. Bile burned the back of my throat. Dominic twitched slightly, just a slight shift of the muscles in his body, but by instinct my mouth opened in preparation to hold him back if he was planning to attack. His eyes turned to slits daring me to say something, and I had no doubt in my mind I'd have a good fight on my hands if I did. What stopped me was not the promise of violence. It was the fact that he stood his ground against someone like Noah. I wanted to bring down the Council. There was no way I could do it alone, and I needed him on my side. The fact that he was easy on the eyes was a bonus I chose to ignore.

Another boom of thunder rattled the windows and the buildings, and that broke my concentration on Dominic. It interrupted my focus on Noah as well, who used that to his advantage. As if forgetting all about killing me and the dagger, he was out through the broken doors faster than my eyes could track him. My hips turned so I could dart after him, but Dominic shifted back to his human form and blocked my way. His size and aura alone made him intimidating at the best of times. Standing naked with the rain splattering behind him and the lightning throwing silver shades over his glistening muscles was intimidation of all new proportions.

I swallowed thickly, unable to hold my eyes on his face. They roamed over his broad shoulders, wide chest, and washboard abs as I hungrily drunk him in. I felt his glare burning a hole in me, but my gaze glided lower to trace the V lines shooting down like an arrow from above his hip bones. Catching myself in time, I snapped my head up and locked my gaze on his now-amused face. It took effort to close my mouth, my tongue sneaking out to wet my suddenly dry lips.

"Noah ..." I croaked through my perched throat.

"I'll track him." The hormones must've hit me hard

86

because I could've sworn his deep voice sounded huskier than before, the rasp in it sending a thrill slithering through me. "You stay here and keep an eye on the human. You lost too much blood."

My ego reared its head. I had less blood left in me when I clawed my way back from the cages. Noah had to die or I was doomed. Shoulders snapping back, I glared at him. "I'll be fine. He needs to die before reaching the Council."

"He will not reach your Council." Turning around, he faced the night through the broken doors. I had to strangle the whimper trying to escape my throat when his back and glutes were presented to me like an offering. Graceful like a cat—pun intended—he strode forward, stopping on the threshold to look at me over his shoulder. "When I get back, we need to talk."

"Hmm?" It took a second to unglue my eyes from his flexing ass to look at his smirking face. "I lost a lot of blood," I blurted out in my defense when I realized I was caught ogling. Again "And be fast." Frowning at him like it was his fault he was built like a statue meant for a museum where he could be freely worshiped, I folded my arms across my chest, wincing from the pain the ripped through me.

"We are in a rush?" One of his eyebrows cocked up, the look turning his face roguishly handsome as a lock of hair fell over his forehead. My fingers itched to reach out and smooth it away.

I fisted my hands.

"If Noah found us, there will be more coming." The words were like a bucket of water over my libido. "If we stay here, we're all going to die."

"I will be back before you know it." He was already stepping outside, the rain pouring over him like from a hose.

"Get the human ready so we can leave immediately." I was already turning to do just that when I heard him say, "And then we will talk."

Was it too much to ask that we not talk about it? One look at his face and I had my answer.

Yes. Yes, it was.

Chapter Eleven

By the time I reached the room at the back of the house, I regretted the deal Dominic made with me. He should've handled Alice and I should've gone to deal with Noah. I was not made for this. Calming people down and having them complacent was Veronica's field of expertise. The lump in my throat did its best to choke me, but I pushed it down, blinking away the burning at the back of my eyes. Thinking about her only made me less willing to face the human. Stopping a few feet from the closed door, I leaned one shoulder on the wall and stared at the entrance as if the entire Council was waiting there for me. Alice's voice floated through the wood and tickled my ears.

"Don't be stupid Alice, vampires and people turning into animals is your crazy imagination," she hissed, the frustration evident in her tone. "Right, because you didn't see fangs and damn panthers in your living room like it was a set for a horror movie," she answered herself, which made me frown until I heard the wolf shifter snarling softly, agreeing or disagreeing with her, I couldn't guess which it was from the sound. "If she really was a monster from nightmares, she would've killed me many times by now. I yelled at her all the time … hello … I yelled…" My heart broke when her voice trembled at the end. I didn't want her to be afraid of me, especially when I needed to get her out of here alive.

The sound of shuffling and a few things banging echoed from behind the closed door, and it was followed by more arguments, but this time her words were muffled as if her head was stuck between two of those large pillows. Glancing down at myself, I grimaced at my torn clothing and the drying blood all over me. I had nothing to change into, nor could I go back to my room to take a shower to protect the fragile state of the human, but I had one thing going for me. Backtracking down the hallway, I crossed the room that was trashed from the fight with Noah and stepped outside under the still-pouring rain.

Straining my ears in case someone was approaching, I lifted my face to the sky and let the rain wash away the night. Hot tears mixed with the icy drops sliding down my face, but I ignored them the best I could. Aware of the dagger still buried under broken wood and splinters behind me, I knew I was stalling. Not even the lightning still splitting the sky or the booming thunder could force me inside to look at Alice. Would she see me, Brooklyn, or would she see the monster she was referring to while talking to herself? It made no difference one way or another because I could tell her to do anything and she would have no choice but to listen. But I didn't want that. I didn't want her to hate me.

It would mean I was just like the rest of my kind.

Keeping my eyes closed and my face turned skyward, I pretended I didn't hear her cautious steps when she approached the front doors, the wolf padding softly over the debris behind her. It irked me that the coward continued to pretend he was an animal, which saved him from whatever fear or disgust Alice felt toward us. A pang in my chest followed her whispered words.

"Brooklyn?" The catch in her voice felt like a knife twisted between my ribs.

I said nothing, the rain peppering my face like tiny needles.

"Brooklyn," Alice hissed fearfully as she leaned on the doorframe. I brought my face down to look at her. "Where are the ... the others?"

Her eyes looked too big on her face, while her long hair was sticking in all directions and the thick frames of her glasses were barely holding on to the tip of her nose. She blinked owlishly, her gaze darting all around me as if waiting for something to jump at her out of nowhere. Her throat worked as she swallowed and the pulse in her neck was thrumming like butterfly wings.

My fangs throbbed in my gums, and that reminded me just how much blood I'd actually lost.

I forced my eyes from her neck to her face.

"There is no one near your home." I wanted to kick myself when my words came out with a lisp, draining what little color had returned to her face. "Don't be afraid of me, Alice. I won't hurt you."

Her pulse picked up and the hunger twisting my stomach called me a liar.

"What are you?" Alice breathed as she took a step back.

"Atua," I answered simply, my words bringing her eyebrows down like an arrow pointing at her nose.

"A what-a?" Shaking her head, she came out of the confusion and the Alice I know peeked through the fright- ened woman in front of me. "Don't talk in riddles, Brooklyn, it's annoying. You have fangs," she said as if I was unaware of that fact and had no idea what was inside my mouth.

"I do, yes." The rain was like icicles hitting my skin, and I shivered but didn't move in case I scared her into running. "I've had them since I was born. I had them the day you met me, and every day after that."

"That makes you a vampire, Brooklyn, not a whatever amataua you said."

"Atua," I corrected her on a sigh. "Vampires don't exist—"

"Right, cause I'm not talking to one…"

"It's a human, made-up creature."

"You have fangs." She was the last one to finish talking, and when she did she held both her forefingers pointed down in front of her mouth as if I had no clue what fangs were. She even wiggled them to make her point.

"I can walk in the daylight." Which wasn't a big lie. We could, we were just sluggish and felt like falling asleep on our feet. The sun made us weak, but that was all.

"There is a name for that type of vampire too …"

"I'm not affected by garlic, holy water, crosses, or your religious buildings. And as you know, I can come inside your home without an invitation. We are not vampires." My hand clenched into a fist when she sunk her fingers into the shifter's fur and absentmindedly scratched the asshole like a pet.

"So how do you die?" When my eyebrow jerked up, she gasped and slapped her hand over her mouth. "I didn't mean it the way it sounded, it's not like I want to kill you, geez." Her words were muffled through her fingers.

"By cutting their throat and ripping their heart out."

Dominic's deep voice rumbled as he stepped under the light of the streetlamp.

Alice shrieked, which made me wince.

She was about to dart inside until her eyes fell and she realized he was naked. All fear forgotten, including my fangs, she stood gawking. Her arm dropped away from the wolf, who growled in protest, and with parted lips, she pushed the glasses up her nose and gave him a leisured once-over. Undisturbed by both Alice and me checking him out like a piece of meat, Dominic sauntered down the street, only stopping when he was level with me. It made me feel better that I wasn't the only one tracing the raindrops that were following each line of muscles that moved gracefully with every step he took.

"Holy shit ..." Alice muttered under her breath, and I had to agree. Silently, of course. It was obvious the shifter didn't need his ego stroked more than it had already been.

"Noah?"

"Will not be a problem anymore." Dominic answered my question, but he kept his gaze on Alice with a frown on his face. "Is she ready? We are running out of time."

"I didn't get a chance to talk to her about leaving." The incredulous look he gave me was well deserved, but I shrugged a shoulder unwilling to explain myself to him. "Her whole life was turned upside down, so she's still in shock," I finished lamely, because if anything, Alice looked very much not shocked and more alert than ever.

"Human, pack your stuff. We need to go," Dominic barked at her, making her jump a foot of the floor.

"Who you calling human, you asshole?" Alice came back to her old self but inched sideways to hide most of her body behind the wall holding the doorframe as if that would protect her from him. "Are you a vampire, too?"

"Atua, and no," I answered for him on a sigh.

A muscle jumped in Dominic's jaw.

"Great, because you are Brooklyn." This apparently gave her courage because she fully stepped out on the tiny porch. "Bite him for being an ass and thinking he can boss us around." When both Dominic and I gaped at her, she nodded her head encouragingly at me. "Do it. Bite him."

"Oh for fucks sake, she thinks you are her pet now, too." Taking a menacing step toward her, he growled the next part with so much fury I took a step away from him. "Her kind kill the rest of us for sport, human. It'll do you good to remember that."

"Brooklyn said she won't hurt me." Lifting her chin, she stood her ground. Warmth spread under my frozen skin. She believed me, and that thought almost made my knees buckle from relief.

"Alice, we need to go because more will come." I spoke to stop the argument that was leading nowhere, and I didn't want to give Dominic a chance to say something that will make her fear me again. "Please, just get what you need and what's important to you. I promise I'll answer all your questions later." I could see the war inside her mind by the way her eyes darted between Dominic and me. So, I told her the truth behind the reason I came here in the first place. "I don't want you to die. I already lost one friend. Don't make me lose another … please."

My heart was trying to punch a hole through my chest when Dominic's head turned slowly my way, his gaze drilling into the side of my face. Keeping my eyes steady on Alice, I flared my nostrils so I could calm my breathing. It was stupid showing weakness in front of him, and I knew that, but I wanted Alice to live more. I'd just have to deal with the fallout from running my mouth later. Much, much later if I had any say in it.

Alice nodded and bolted inside to grab her things, which left us standing in the rain. Both of us kept an eye on things, our gazes bouncing off the buildings and up and down the street in case they came before we had the chance to get a running start. I was uncomfortable that Dominic was standing so close to me, and the heat wafting off his body seared my chilled skin. What was it about him that made me acutely aware of his presence even when he was nowhere to be found? That night when I found the dead woman came to mind, so I gave him a side-eyed glance.

"Have you been following me around?"

"You think too highly of yourself, princess. If I followed you around, you'd be dead by now." He didn't even grace me with a look when he said it. "Did you get the dagger?"

"No."

Reminded of the blade, I mumbled my answer before darting inside to fetch it. There was no need to look through all the mess that was in the room. The dagger called to me like a siren song, so I shuffled my feet closer until I stood on top of it. A piece of the broken door covered half of it, so I nudged it with my boot to reveal the weapon. The rain eased out a little, the peppering of the raindrops on the roof matching my heartbeat. Noah's words came uninvited and they echoed through my head. *"It used to belong to your father. He didn't get much of a chance to use it."* With a shaking hand, I reached for it. Then I picked it up, letting its weight settle comfortably in the palm of my hand. I was turning it slowly to see the blade better when Alice came behind me, and she was much closer than I expected. Especially after she had seen the monster I actually was.

"That looks like an athame." My emotions mirrored the fascination in her tone.

"And you know this how?" Tucking the blade in the empty holster on my thigh, I turned to face her while motioning that we need to move.

"Just because I didn't know vampires existed doesn't mean I don't know anything." Huffing, she stomped through the room and tossed what looked like a large satchel over her shoulder, the wolf back again by her side. The damn shifter hid in the back while we were fighting like the coward he was. "I know what it is because I'm a witch."

Tripping over nothing, I pitched forward and was barely able to stop myself from falling on the floor. I was well aware that Alice was human and not a witch, but hearing her say it was like a punch to the stomach. I'd watched humans for a long time because I found them fascinating, but I also envied the freedom they didn't know they had. But what did I really know about them? Maybe Alice could help me even more now, especially if she knew things I was not aware of. If I wanted to bring the Council down, I could use all the help I could get.

Dominic met us at the door, his large-but-still-very-naked frame blocking the light coming from the street. His eyes flicked from Alice to me, and he cocked an eyebrow in question, which meant he had obviously been eavesdropping on our conversation. Alice spun in a circle when she saw him coming behind me and gripped the back of my shirt in her fisted hand. The fact that she was afraid of him and not me made up for the shitty day I'd had, at least a little. The wolf snarled stepping between us and the panther shifter.

"A witch?" The doubt was obvious in his deep voice and he ignored the wolf completely.

"I'm sure it doesn't mean to her what it means to us." Sidestepping the wolf and ushering Dominic in front of me, we joined him in the rain. "Would it kill you to put on some clothes?"

"Don't listen to her. She's just a prude," Alice muttered as she stabbed her knuckles into my back.

"Unless you let me borrow yours, I didn't bring anything else to put on." Ignoring the human, he smirked at me.

"Where are we going?" Weary to the bones and still slightly lightheaded from blood loss, I blinked the rain out of my eyes and peeked through my lashes at the shifter.

"We can use my parents' house if you like." It was Alice who answered, her words making Dominic and me turn to face her. "They died a few years ago, so I haven't been there much, but it's kind of out of the way." When we just stared at her, she snorted a crazed laugh that bubbled out of her mouth. "I don't want to die either, Brooklyn. And the way I see it, the two of you aren't gunning for my throat. I have a better chance of surviving whatever is coming with you than I do alone."

"I'll be damned, the human has a brain," Dominic drawled, and that only earned him a blistering glare from the said human.

"The only thing going for you is that swinging penis, so what's your point?" she challenged, hefting the satchel higher on her shoulder.

I laughed.

And I couldn't stop the burst of laughter that bubbled out of me, not even if my life depended on it. Leave it to Alice to call him out on his attitude while chipping at his ego. She had a way of leaving you speechless while wondering if she was really that brave or she just had no sense of self preservation. That was what made me like her in the first place.

"You two get in my car. I'll be right back." Shoving the satchel at my chest, she was already entering the house before I could call her back.

Shrugging a shoulder at the glaring shifter, I walked up to the beat-up pickup truck and tried not to rip the door off when I opened it. The thing looked one bolt away from falling apart. We didn't have to spend a long time wondering where Alice went. All the barking and screeching coming closer made it clear enough. The human was taking all the animals with her, which had me grinning at Dominic.

The feline was not happy about it.

I was going to enjoy the ride.

Chapter Twelve

For two days after arriving at the small farmhouse a few miles outside Chicago, I avoided Dominic like the plague, pretending to be busy by helping Alice situate all the animals she brought with us. I also made sure the building could withstand an assault in case they found us. He was busy himself, constantly shifting out of sight and prowling the perimeter to ensure our safety.

We weren't safe.

Nor would we ever be unless I did something. That still didn't mean I was ready, not in any shape or form, to face the shifter and answer his questions. I expected him to corner me and demand to hear the truth the second we stopped the rattling pickup truck, but to my surprise and even though he'd been eyeing me strangely since then, he never breached the subject. It suited me fine, at least until I realized I had questions of my own. Watching him move around like the earth should bow to him for gracing her with his weight on her soil was a small worm eating at me, too, and it only made curiosity burn hot inside my brain.

Who was this male?

What insanity made him enter a nest of Atua, not once but twice, and save my life in the process. Hatred and resentment followed that thought because why hadn't he come sooner. Then maybe he could've saved Veronica's life too. Could he have done it? Would he have done it? And the most important question of them all ...

Why me?

What made *me* worth saving but not my friend.

Dominic was already wary of me, the distrust evident in his every action. I pushed all those questions aside so I didn't lose my mind. Focusing on Alice and rebuilding her trust in me was my priority. Human or not, she was my ace in this game. I had to have a solid plan to destroy the Syndicate, and I only had one chance. If things went sideways, there might be a chance that Alice could get me to one of the reservations. If a Shaman allowed passage, Atua would be able to pass the protections they had around their lands. How true that was, I wasn't sure, but it was worth a try. So, I needed her calm and well if I was to proceed with my plans.

"Brooklyn?" Alice called from inside the house.

I kept my gaze on the surrounding trees hiding the property from the main road. A narrow path made by moving vehicles sneaked through them, and it led to the gravel that was poured at the front of the house to create an open space to park and nothing else. The wide wooden porch where I stood leaning on the banister wrapped around the small home, two rocking chairs and a swinging two-seater the only furniture on it. Alice brought them out when we'd arrived and said the house felt wrong if they were not where they were supposed to be. It made me think of my parents.

I didn't know my mother and I had vague memories of my father. Every time I tried to remember anything specific or recall a time I'd spent with him, no matter how far in the past it was, a splitting headache would almost bring me to my knees. I knew something was off about it but never cared. Not until Noah pulled out that dagger and mentioned my father. There must be more to it than just him dying to protect the Council, that much I knew.

The tension in my temples started throbbing with just those thoughts, so I shook my head to clear my mind. It wasn't worth the suffering, and at the end it didn't really matter. I couldn't bring my father back from the dead, but I could kill Isiah, Frederic, and Samir. To kill a snake, all you had to do was cut off its head. The three of them had ruled over us for as far back as I could remember, and their cruelty and evil had spread like a virus among the Atua. Their egos made them micromanage the Syndicate to the point that no one loyal to the Council could think for themselves. I was going to take advantage of that if it was the last thing I did. They had just made one mistake: they were so hungry for power that everyone who showed even the slight promise of it had been eliminated without even the blink of an eye.

Or so they thought.

In three years, I had over a dozen shifters hidden inside the reservation. Granted I hadn't been polite or nice about it, and I definitely hadn't given them the option to refuse, but they were alive because of me. That had to count for something. If they agreed to help me, there was no doubt in my mind that I could bring the Syndicate down on its knees. They would pay for more than just Veronica's death. The problem I was facing was how to get them to trust me. I couldn't get Dominic to look at me without glaring, so how in the world would I convince more than a dozen or so? Lost in my thoughts, I didn't hear Alice walking outside to join me until she spoke.

"How old are you?" She didn't look at me as she leaned over the banister next to me, her gaze tracing the line of trees.

"Older than I look. Why?" That was the wrong thing to say because she pursed her lips, jerkily pushing her glasses up her nose with a stiff forefinger.

"Must be over ninety because you are losing your hearing." Turning her head to finally look at me, her lips stretched into a wide smile at my frown. "Next thing you know, *grandma*, you'll be senile. You'll need my help so you don't wander off and get hit by a car or something."

"I fail to see the humor in this. We are still considered younglings at ninety …" I trailed off when her eyebrows crawled all the way to her hairline. "Was there a point to your question?"

"I called you numerous times, but you didn't hear me." Fully turning her body my way, she propped a hip on the banister while nervously playing with the bracelets on her wrists. "I've been dying to ask questions, but I'm worried that I might piss you off and … you know …" she mimicked a mouth with her hand and snapped at her neck.

I blinked at her.

"In case you didn't understand, that was in case you get made and decide I'm not worth keeping around because I'm annoying and you chew on my neck to get rid of me." Rolling her eyes, she acted like I was dumb for not understanding her pantomime.

"There are other parts I could chew on that would keep you alive longer and prolong your suffering." My mouth snapped shut when her face blanched, and then her body sagged heavily on the banister like her legs were unable to hold her. "Alice …" My hand reached out to catch her in case she crumbled, but I dropped it to my side when she flinched with a wide-eyed look on her face. "I'm sorry, I didn't mean I would do it. Sometimes I say things before I think them through."

"You think?" Her voice shook, but she recovered quickly, impressing me with the strength of her character.

The Syndicate was all I knew, and to survive in that snake pit I'd always had to speak as cruelly as possible. I had to make sure there was no emotion attached to my statements, else I wouldn't be taken seriously. More importantly, so I wasn't messed with. When dealing with a human, I had no idea how to hold a conversation without scaring the life out of her. Seeing Alice occasionally to make sure the shifters were transported safely was one thing. Being around her day and night was a whole new hell, and it was one I'd never had time to prepare for.

The sound of tires crunching the fallen branches and pebbles pinging off the bottom of the pickup truck announced Dominic's return. We both turned at the sound and watched the vehicle bounce over the driveway, and we didn't miss the large male gripping the steering wheel in both hands as if trying to strangle it. His face was relaxed, which turned his harsh features softer. I couldn't help but admire how handsome he actually was. That was until he saw me. His jaw clenched and his eyes narrowed until the familiar suspicious stare I was accustomed to clicked into place. Even his knuckles tightened around the steering wheel.

"Who pooped in his cereal?" Alice muttered while adjusting her glasses. "That man is as annoying as winding a yo-yo backwards, twisting it in knots, and trying to untangle it. Would it kill him to smile? All he does is glare and snap at both of us."

"He doesn't trust me. You have nothing to do with it." I coughed, but only to cover up the laugh threatening to escape at her description. She wasn't wrong.

"Did you do something to him?" she asked just as Dominic was exiting the truck, which made him pause halfway out the door.

"Me personally?" For some stupid reason I felt a blush creeping into my cheeks. "No, I haven't done anything." She took a deep breath, no doubt to say something else that would make me want to run and hide, so I rushed to silence her. "But my kind must've done something. It wouldn't surprise me if they did."

"So?" Undeterred by the now glaring shifter that was still frozen halfway out of the driver's seat, she continued staring pointedly at him. No self-preservation whatsoever. "By that logic, every human should want to kill one another as soon as we see each other. Do you know how many crazies have done psychotic things in this world? Atrocious, unspeakable things to other human beings. I can't hate all humankind because of a few bad apples."

"That is kind of you to say, Alice." Giving her a grateful smile, I flinched when Dominic slammed the door with so much force I thought the truck would fall apart. "But our worlds are different. He has every right not to trust me or like me because of what I am. I don't blame him for that."

"That's you. I can blame him all I want." She kept raising her voice until she shouted the last part at his retreating back. "Asshole." Huffing in annoyance, she shook her head at me as if saying *'Can you believe that?'*

Making sure he was out of ear shot, I tugged on her

arm so she paid attention. Keeping my voice as low as I could so she could still hear me, I bent my head closer to hers. "Don't anger him, Alice. Dominic is very calm and I'm very happy he is on our side making sure none of my kind get anywhere near this place. You need to remember that he is not human."

"You said he is not a vampire." She threw at me accusingly.

"Atua, and no he is not. This is the second time you compared him to me. Why?"

"He was fighting that panther in my kennel." Her frame shivered as she remembered that night.

Frowning, I recalled the fight and realized she could've mistaken the two males in the darkness since they had the same color hair and similar height. Her human sight was not as good as ours, and that didn't even count how scared out of her mind she had probably been and the glasses she wore, so it would've been difficult to tell the difference.

"What?" When I didn't answer fast enough to her liking, she actually tugged on my arm. "What?" she repeated, and I decided I wasn't going to lie to her.

"Dominic wasn't fighting the panther in your building, Alice."

"What do you mean? Yes he was." My heart bumped hard against my breastbone at her worried, confused face.

"No, he wasn't fighting it." Locking my gaze on hers, I braced for the reaction. "Dominic was the panther."

"Brooklyn?" Alice whimpered, her body leaning heavily on the banister. "I think I'm going to pass out now."

I snatched her unconscious body before it hit the porch. Cradling her in my arms, I turned to take her inside but a movement from the corner of my eye stopped me in my tracks. Dominic was watching me from the side of the house, his gaze swiping up and down my body with an expression I couldn't name.

"Take the human inside. We need to have that talk."

Lovely, that was exactly what I needed.

A talk with a pissed-off shifter.

Chapter Thirteen

A guilt I wasn't aware I carried for everything the Syndicate had done weighed on my shoulders, and I slouched as I dragged my feet out of the house after leaving Alice as comfortable as I could make her on the couch in the small living room. The clothing I borrowed from her stretched a little tight around my shoulders and chest, so I snatched the thick sweater hanging on a hook by the door as I closed it softly behind me. There was a bite in the air that smelled like incoming rain, so I wrapped my arms around my torso like a shield, hugging the knitted garment that hung down to my thighs. We didn't feel the elements as bad as humans did, but we were not immune to them either. Something they forgot to tell Dominic, who was pacing up and down the side of the house wearing a new path around it with his boots. I felt sorry for the crushed grass under the soles of his feet.

And, how nice of him to grab some of his clothing while he was out patrolling.

The faded t-shirt he wore was hanging on for dear life

around his muscular frame, the seams ready to burst at any second every time he clenched his fists and his biceps bulged like balloons. As agitated as he was, the stomping he was doing shouldn't have looked graceful or hot as hell, but it did. My tongue stuck to the roof of my mouth. Staying silent, I approached him, my mind racing with what I should say and how to handle him. I almost laughed at the thought of anyone handling Dominic. The male was as wild and as untamed as they came. The civil façade he presented to the outside world crumbled like dominoes the moment I looked at his eyes. There was something primal and savage there, daring me to challenge it. Leaning one shoulder on the wall with peeling paint flaking off it, I stood waiting and tracked his every move.

"I wanted to ask what you've done that your Council," he spat the word as if it tasted vile in his mouth, "would want to kill you, but I saw the evidence myself when I followed you to the human."

He didn't look at me or stop pacing, so I waited, tracing every move and every expression crossing his downturned face. Confusion mixed with the anger puckering his brow, which only added to the dominant air he exuded around him. He took up more space in this world than anyone had any right to do.

Who was this guy?

"I had every intention of killing you when I took you from that damn place." His gaze bore into mine, so intent I found it hard to breathe. Lucky for me I had to learn not to show any expression when faced with a crazed male. "I don't know why I didn't."

That last part was pushed through clenched teeth like an accusation. Like it was my fault he couldn't go through with it. We stared at each other for a long time, none of us uttering a word, but I was lost for what to say to that. What could I say? Thank you for not killing me? Try harder next time?

"You can compel your own kind." And there it was, the one thing I hoped he would skip in this talk of his. "What are you?" The menacing step he took toward me made my heart jump to my throat and lodge there.

"Atua," I answered him evenly with no infliction in my voice. "What else could I be?"

One second he was wound up as tight as a rubber band ready to snap and glaring at me from a few feet away, and the next the wall of the house crumbled over my shoulders, his fists embedded in it on both sides of my head. The heat from his body scolded my skin, and his furious panted breaths wafted across my face until my nostrils were filled with his scent. My senses were overwhelmed.

"Don't try to lie to me, female." Each snarled word brought his lips closer to mine, and that caused my breath to hitch. "Is this a new trick that they've started testing so they can get to me?"

"I'm a little lost now." Working hard to maintain my calm demeanor, I couldn't stop my eyebrows from lifting in surprise. What the hell was he talking about?

"For years I've been picking you off one by one, giving myself time to find a way to rid the world of the vermin that you are."

He paused as if expecting me to be offended by the insult, but I just stared unblinking at his rage-twisted face. My mind was also stuck on what he'd actually said. He had been killing off Atua and not a word had spilled out through the Syndicate. I shouldn't have been shocked that the Council would do everything to cover that up, to hide their weakness. Yet I was. This only cemented my decision to gain his trust, as impossible as it might sound, because if he could get to them, I could get to them through him.

"And here you are, still breathing." I flinched when he growled deep in his chest at the end of that statement. A cruel smile lifted one corner of his mouth at my reaction.

"What did my kind do to you, Dominic?" Saying his name was my attempt to calm him down enough to hear me, and it worked for a split second because that was the wrong question to ask. The story of my life.

"What they always do!" Dominic roared in my face, punching the wall next to my head again. His voice carried through the trees around us. Birds screeched in the distance, a flock of them soaring into the night sky like a dark cloud.

I wished I could be one of them.

"They will destroy anything that doesn't further their agenda or has no purpose to them." Seeing the predator staring at me through his now-glowing electric green eyes was fascinating enough that I had to tighten my arms around me so I didn't reach out and touch his face. For some idiotic reason, I had an urge to smooth the strained lines with my fingers and make whatever put them there go away. "Fates forbid anyone lives that has enough power to stand up against all the heinous things they are doing to the rest of us."

There it was, plain as a sunny day. I never wanted to see the reason he hated me so much. I should've known. "Who did you lose?"

"You don't get to gloat at that, vermin." This time I did move, slapping the palm of my hand at the center of his chest because he looked like he was about to bite my head off.

He pressed harder on my hand as if testing my strength and how far I would go.

"Unless you suffer from short-term memory loss, I lost my best friend a few days ago." He bared his teeth at me, reminding me he could shift at any moment and it wouldn't be fun to fight his panther. I could reason with the man, not with the animal. "She was the only family I had left."

His angry gaze dropped to the pendant sitting inconspicuously on my throat before flicking back to mine.

"I didn't get to choose what I was born into." Puffing out a deep sigh, I started doubting that we would ever come to see eye to eye on anything. The hatred was so deeply embedded in Dominic that a saint would be named a sinner without judgment day.

Not that I was a saint.

"I can't physically take it off." Which is one thing that truly bothered me about the night Veronica had been killed. How did she remove it? "It's spelled to mark us as Syndicate, which I'm sure you know."

I held my breath when his arm lifted, his fingers grazing my skin when they wrapped around the chain. They curled tightly around the necklace, and without looking away from my eyes, Dominic started pulling on it. A crazy thought entered my head that he might actually do it, but it was gone just as fast when the chain cut into my skin and sent pain shooting across my shoulders and to the base of my skull. With clenched teeth, I endured it while still holding his gaze, unable to hide the hope sparking in my chest. *Do it. Do it*, my mind encouraged him until tears started burning the back of my eyes.

"My entire family." His deep voice came out so soft I felt the words in the palm pressed to his chest more than I heard them.

"What?" The pain was clouding my mind, his forearm still flexing in his attempt to rip the pendant off me.

"They killed my whole family." So many emotions flickered through his green eyes that I forgot all about my own pain and suffering.

"For what it's worth, I'm sorry." Not even in his fury could he deny the sincerity in my voice, which took him aback. "I was born into the Syndicate, but I never agreed with their lifestyle or methods."

Dominic stared at me like he was seeing me for the first time, his hand dropping to his side and releasing the chain he was tugging on. I knew this was my one chance to penetrate the preconceived perspective he had of me, so I decided to tell him the truth. Not all of it, but enough so he could see in me as more than just a heartless Syndicate Atua.

"I never knew my mother, and I was very young when I lost my father. Raised like the vermin you call me, I did all I could to survive. I never killed out of cruelty, only to protect myself." Seeing his eyes narrow, I pushed through so he didn't cut me off. "Yes, I have killed. And so have you, so don't you dare judge me. That was until someone befriended me and I foolishly believed I could trust them. To cut a long story short, who I believed to be my friend turned out to be someone sent to keep an eye on me. The Council wanted to know my every thought, every action, every word spoken out of my mouth …"

My body trembled slightly from the onslaught of memories, so I pulled my hand away from his chest so he didn't notice. To my surprise, Dominic's hand took hold of my forearm as if offering courage to continue. Not wanting to see sadness or, fates forbid, pity in his eyes at the next part, I stared over his shoulder, my unseeing eyes clouded with what came next.

"I abhor violence." A humorless laugh burst through my

lips. "A pathetic example of my kind, don't you think?" He stayed silent, so I continued. "The Council said I was ready to go up the chain one night. I dreaded the day, and after centuries I believed it might never happen. But it did. It was a week after I stupidly stood up for someone when they were being cornered. My friend was with me, and it was his idea to help. I believed him. So, the Council decided that my way of stepping up should be for me to kill the only friend I had. It was how we show our loyalty is only to the Syndicate, you see."

"You killed your friend." This time there was no accusation in Dominic's voice. No, it was worse. He felt sorry for me. My eyes locked on his for a moment.

"No, I didn't kill him." He couldn't hide the shock fast enough for me not to see it. "Johnathan is very much alive, even today. I told him to run. Even went as far as finding places where he could hide and I can go later to help him disappear."

"They found out?"

"He told them, actually." Rolling my shoulders to shake off the tension, I slid my back on the wall because it was getting stiff from standing still for so long. "I was sent to the cages." The sharp intake of breath told me Dominic was well aware of the place the Council used if they wanted to prolong your death. "Johnathan, on the other hand, became their most trusted pet."

"No one escapes the cages." The distrust was back in his baritone, and it rubbed me wrong.

"Yeah, well, meet no one. It's a pleasure to meet your acquaintance," I deadpanned sardonically. "Anyway, I clawed my way out of that nightmare, and since then I did good convincing them I was ready to do anything they wanted so I would never be sent back there again. All my jobs from that day were shifters, and so far every single one of them is still breathing, as far as I'm aware."

"If you are telling me this so I don't kill you, you didn't need to waste your breath." Turning away from me, he stared across the tree line, taking away his scent with him, which was helping to calm me. "I don't trust you, but that's not enough reason for me to take a life." *Unlike my kind* was left hanging unsaid in the air between us. "All of you that I have killed deserved it. I was waiting until I caught them in the act before ridding the world of the plague they were."

My mind went back to the night I first felt his scent. "You were there that night." It also meant he saved my life twice if he killed whoever followed me there and killed that woman. "It was you watching me and Alice when we found the body."

"You didn't kill the human, so you lived."

"How very noble of you."

"Why?" Ignoring my snark, he glanced at me over his shoulder.

"Why what?"

"Why did you tell me all of that if not to stop me from killing you?"

Wiping my sweat-covered palms on my borrowed pants, I plunged through with my decision. "You have an insider in the Syndicate, and you can get in and out without being killed. I know you are not willing to share details but… I need your help."

"For what exactly?"

"I'm going to bring the Syndicate down, but I want them to suffer first." Dominic slowly turned to face me at my fevered words. "I want them scared of their own shadow before they meet their maker." Just like I was for as long as I was locked in that cage. The same way Veronica felt before Isiah took her life.

Dominic squinted at me, rubbing his chin in thought. I wasn't sure what he could see on my face, but whatever it was it curled his lips up at the corners and made his green eyes glint in the moonlight peeking through the moving clouds.

"You are planning on becoming a vigilante hunting them down on your own?" The mocking tone he used made me want to slap him.

"Listen asshole, just because I don't see violence as the only option to solve a problem doesn't mean I'm not capable of it. There is a reason that you hate my kind. You can help me, or I'll just do it alone. It makes no difference to me one way or another." But it did make a difference and we both knew it.

"Why do you change the color of your hair like that?" I was so confused all I could do was blink at him like an idiot. "Why do you make it red?" he clarified when I continued staring mutely.

"I was born like this."

"And you claim to be Atua." My nostrils flared in irritation at the way he said that. Like I should be aware that he caught the lie. "None of them have hair like that."

"Thanks, I wasn't aware of that fact."

"I have every intention on finding the truth, Brooklyn." Stretching his arms over his head, he lifted on his toes and his t-shirt climbed up and exposed his rippled stomach. I jerked my eyes away from that to his face to find him smirking. "The second I find a lie, you'll die." Cracking his neck, Dominic's hands went to the belt holding his jeans securely to his waist and he started unbuckling it.

"What are you doing?" I panicked, not because he was

planning to strip while having a conversation like this. I was worried that I wasn't going to be able to stop myself from touching him.

"Getting ready," he told me simply, and then he let his jeans pool at his ankles.

I gawked like a fool.

The arrogant bastard had no underwear on.

"Ready for what?" I muttered, my gaze locked on the bobbing erection between his powerful thighs.

"They found us." That snapped my attention back to his face. "They are coming." It was hard to miss the excitement in those words.

And with that he shifted, leaving me screaming inside my head for allowing him to distract me enough not to notice the air around us change.

The Syndicate was on the land.

Chapter Fourteen

Bolting inside the house, I almost ripped the door off the hinges. It banged loudly on the opposite wall, the frame rattling behind me. The yellow paint on the walls looked dull and faded, but the small home had an air of calm that made you want to curl up in one of the armchairs that had seen better days and just breathe. That feeling was missing when I skidded to a stop looming over Alice's sleeping form. The wolf was curled up on one of her shins, and when I arrived, he growled deep in his throat at me. Taking hold of the skin between his shoulder blades, I flung him at the wall and away from her. I had no time to waste on idiots.

Slinging Alice over my shoulder like a sack of potatoes, I frantically looked around, my gaze bouncing off the pictures of her with her parents hanging on the walls and pinging across the faded furniture and little knickknacks sprinkled over the small fireplace before diving to the shelves and side tables. The door to the kitchen stood slightly open, and I remembered that she showed me the claustrophobic basement where her mother loved keeping canned stuff that she made. It wasn't ideal, but it was better than leaving her out in the open if anyone managed to sneak through Dominic and me.

Rushing across the narrow hallway separating the two rooms, I shouldered my way inside the kitchen and headed straight for the pantry door. It was left open, the shelves still filled with mason jars full of jams and sauces I had no doubt were expired. Alice didn't try to eat them, she just liked watching them, so I kept my opinion to myself. Adjusting her weight on my shoulder, I crouched and curled my fingers under the gap on the wooden floor, yanking the basement door open. It came up soundlessly, leaving a dark pit gaping at my feet. A shiver crawled up my spine when I realized how low the ceiling was and that I'd be standing there surrounded by earth-packed walls and floor.

Like a grave.

The wood protested from our combined weight as I descended, pulling the door closed over my head. Flicking the switch on the side, I had to blink many times when the bright yellow lightbulb buzzed and bathed us in light. Ignoring the damn shifter scratching at the door trying to get in, I lowered Alice on the dirt-covered floor and left her there with a whispered sorry before getting out. That place was creepy as hell, and it brought back memories of closed-up spaces, blood, and metal bars all around me. Still holding my breath, I almost knocked out the wolf when I pushed the plank up to exit.

"Instead of acting like an idiot, you can come help." Hissing at him, I made sure he didn't sneak inside to join the human. "Out of all of you, I'm starting to regret saving your ass."

He bared his sharp teeth at me but stayed out of reach.

Not stupid by any stretch of the imagination.

The house was quiet. Too quiet for my liking, so on silent feet I moved around, flipping off switches as I went and blanketing everything in darkness. A low silvery glow peeked through the lacy white curtains hanging on the windows, giving enough light to break apart the thick shadows. Passing the wooden table and four chairs, I snatched the dagger that was placed on top of it visible for all to see. I left it there so Dominic didn't pitch a fit at me for hiding it so I could slit his throat or something. It came in handy that it was within reach tonight. The weight of it settled in my palm, and I slinked out of the still-open front door, pulling it closed behind me. The wolf stayed on my heels as if he'd decided he had a better chance of surviving outside than locked inside of the house. He had nowhere to hide anyway, because his scent gave him away to any of my kind.

Pausing on the porch, I strained my ears and goosebumps covered my arms when the silence enveloped me in its embrace. Even the crickets that chirped constantly like there was no tomorrow were as quiet as if someone had pressed the mute button. A shadow moved at the start of the tree line, and my heart kicked painfully at my ribs. Dominic's green eyes glinted in the moonlight. Without that, I wouldn't even know he was there because he blended into the darkness. With a nod in his direction, I pushed off the balls of my feet and wrapped my fingers around the lace woodwork decorating the roof of the porch. Flinging my body up, I somersaulted over it and landed in a crouch on the sunburned tiles, my head moving left and right as I searched for any sign of movement. The wolf darted across the few yards of the open area in front of the house, disappearing between the trees. Perched on the roof like some gargoyle, I stayed motionless, waiting. I didn't have long to wait.

A shrill scream split the night.

My eyes flicked to Dominic, who was still standing at the start of the tree line, and the panther grinned broadly, exposing two rows of deadly, sharp teeth. Another roar filled with pain bounced off the thick tree trunks in the sea of green, echoing through the expanse of land. Whatever the shifter had done around the property had ensured we had a head start, but it also made the Atua realize we knew they had arrived.

Tree tops and branches swayed all of a sudden, and whatever had disturbed them was coming at us full speed from three sides. Not taking away my eyes from it, I pointed in each direction, knowing that Dominic was waiting for it. It was strange how in sync I felt with someone I hadn't known longer than a week. He weaved through the trees until he picked one side, his long, thick tail snapping once in the air before going out of sight. The wolf looped out in the open for a few feet before heading in the opposite direction of Dominic. I stayed on the roof, tracking whoever was coming right at me, my hand tightening on the dagger and my fangs throbbing in my gums.

Three figures emerged from the trees and stepped into the open.

There was no mistaking the guards of the Council, their bare torsos glistening in the moonlight as they fanned out in hopes to surround the house. My scent was thick here, so I wasn't surprised they thought I'd be hiding inside. Everything they'd seen of me indicated that I should be afraid of the Syndicate. And I was, just not enough to stop me from wanting to tear their throats out. Before they had a chance to move out of sight, I dropped from the roof, making sure I made enough noise for all three of them to hear me. Three sets of eyes locked on my frame, the feeling of it forming an itch on my skin.

"How nice of you to visit," I drawled, shifting slightly to have all three in my field of vision. "If you would've sent word before you came, I could've baked you cookies."

"The Council requests your presence if you want to live." The one facing me grumbled, his voice grating on my nerves like rocks grinding together.

I almost laughed. The scream coming from somewhere in the trees strangled the sound in my throat.

"Okay, go back and tell them I'll come." The puckering of his forehead was comical. "I just need to take a shower and do my makeup."

"You'll come?" The hand gripping a wicked-looking carved short sword dropped slightly while he gawked at me.

"She's not coming, you idiot." The guard from the left snarled and glared at his friend.

"Aww, I see it now. The three amigos, am I right?" Grinning, I pointed the tip of my dagger at each of them in turn. "The Brains, The brawn, and ..." I glanced at the third, who looked like he was flabbergasted by our little conversation. "You should be the booty, I think. They'll need a little somethin' somethin' while on the road."

That did it.

They came at me from three sides like freight trains playing chicken. I stood still and waited. When the first weapon lifted in the air, I dropped on the ground and rolled out of the way. Having just enough time to get back on my feet, my dagger clashed with a carved sword, my arm straining to hold it back from my face. The asshole was aiming right for my head. Spinning on my heel, I released the pressure and the guard's body pitched forward, so I elbowed him in the back of his head as hard as I could. He dropped on the ground with a growl, but another replaced him while he was busy eating dirt.

I moved in a circle around the one at my feet, fighting the two still standing, who of course were hell bent on killing me. Every time the first one tried to lift himself, I'd kick him as hard as I could to keep him there. The guilt and grief for Veronica bubbled to the surface, and this time I allowed my emotions to burst forward until they bathed everything in a red haze. I wanted to kill them, and I wanted to make it as prolonged as possible. The hilt of the dagger radiated heat in my palm, and it was as if my rage was its own.

A switch flipped in my brain and calmness bathed me from the inside. My body moved without conscious thought, kicking, punching, and slicing anything I could reach. The pain burning where they managed to get a hit was a distant feeling, as if it was happening to someone else. Every roar or shout—along with a few screams—was music to my ears. I kept slicing with my dagger, taking every opportunity to tear flesh with my fangs when that I could. It must've started raining, but strangely the raindrops peppering my face were warm when I felt them sliding down to my neck.

One of the guards took hold of the thick sweater I stupidly forgot to take off and yanked me toward him, his blade sliding into my side like through butter. Fire erupted where I'd been stabbed, and I screamed so loud he released me to cover his ears. A mistake that cost him his life, because my dagger found his throat and I slashed so harshly I almost severed his head. The guard dropped in a pile of limbs at my feet and I stumbled over him, almost falling on my ass. This gave the one still on the ground time to roll away and jump to his feet. His face was all bloody, his cheekbones crushed from the many times I stomped on his head to keep him out of the fight.

"Kill him," I told the guard who'd been fighting me this whole time.

Without a pause, the guard turned to his friend's body and stabbed the carved sword through his eye. The shocked expression on the now-dead guard's face was frozen for eternity while I watched the other one punch his fist through his chest and rip his heart out. Keeping an eye on him, I kneeled and did the same to the guard at my feet. I let the heart drop on the ground with a sickening plop and blinked at the only one left standing. Screams still echoed from the trees, which told me Dominic was having his own fun encounter.

"Now rip your own heart out," I told the remaining guard, and with horror plastered all over his face, he stared at his own hand obeying my command.

His body joined the other two around me, and pressing a hand to the still-bleeding wound, I stumbled away from them in hopes to reach the porch. My legs felt heavy, and the world was spinning around me like a carousel. The tips of my boots scraped the pebbled ground and I fell over the porch steps until I sprawled over them resembling roadkill. With effort, I rolled on my back staring at a moldy patch on the roof above me. It was blurry as hell, so I blinked furiously to clear my vision as if the mold would clear if only I could see it better.

A slow loud clap jerked my body up.

"I must say, very impressive, Brooklyn." Johnathan pushed off the tree he was leaning on and headed toward me with an even, measured gait, clapping. "You are full of surprises, aren't you? No wonder the Council is willing to have everyone killed as long as they get their hands on you."

My attempt at standing up so I could kill him failed miserably when I dropped back on my ass, bruising my tail-bone on the wooden steps. My hand gripped the railing so I didn't pitch forward and start eating dirt at his feet like the vermin Dominic told me I was. Where was he anyway? Was he still alive? Dear fates, I hope so because Alice was still in the house. That sent panic through me, and it was enough to force me on my feet.

"Johnathan, I should've expected you here. Wherever I smell something foul, a piece of shit like you pops up." My words were slurred, but the glare on his face told me I did well.

"You will learn to obey, Brooklyn." I didn't like the glint in his eyes, so I gripped the banister tighter so I didn't sway on my feet like a drunk. Blood oozed lazily through the fingers of my hand, I've lost so much of it that it couldn't gush even if it wanted to. "I'll make sure of it."

"Over my dead body, asshole," I venomously spat at him while wishing I could wrap my hands around his neck and rip his head off.

"Oh, but you will." Now almost within arm's reach, he snickered like an idiot. "And it will be a joy to teach you obedience. The more you fight, the sweeter the reward will be."

"Come closer then. We should seal it with a kiss." When he didn't do what I asked, I frowned at his grinning face. "Come closer." I tried again with no result.

My heart was sluggishly drumming against my chest.

Reaching in his pocket, he pulled out something that looked like an amulet dangling between his fingers on a leather cord. Bringing it in the air between us, he didn't stop smiling like the fool that he was.

"I knew I had a reason to make the witches create

124

protection for compulsion. But enough talking, we need to go."

I braced for a fight I knew I couldn't win and watched his hand coming to snatch me in slow motion. My brain was screaming at me to move, kick, or even bite him, but the order never reached my frozen limbs. Terror threatened to choke me. I couldn't go back to the Council. I couldn't.

A feral, ferocious cry pebbled my skin, and a dark shadow like death himself was flying at me burst from the trees. Johnathan jerked back wide eyed, his face blanching before he turned around, and in less time than I could blink, he was gone. All my strength left me the second green glowing eyes locked on mine. The panther seemed larger than life hunching protectively in front of me, blood matting his smooth fur. For some stupid reason, I smiled.

I'm safe, my inner voice announced before my eyes rolled to the back of my head.

The last thing I remembered was not hitting the hard, wooden steps. Instead, my body molded over warm silky fur.

Chapter Fifteen

Distant voices pulled at my subconscious, dragging me out kicking and screaming from the blissful darkness that surrounded me. I didn't want to leave that place where I felt nothing but calm. There, not even the memories from the cages surfaced, and I wanted to stay so badly my mind raged in protest. Something was poking at my lips insistently, and I tried to swat it away but my arm wouldn't move. My belly felt full too, instead of caving in on itself like the last couple of days.

"That is not how it's done, human." Dominic's deep voice came through loud and clear, but the frustration in it every time he spoke around me or Alice was missing. He almost sounded worried.

"If you have a better idea, go ahead, I'm all ears," Alice snapped at him, her voice coming from right above my head. "If not, go sit there and let me do my thing. I mean, how hard can it be?"

The feeling was slowly returning to my numbed limbs, but I still couldn't open my eyes to see what was going on.

My mouth didn't want to move either. Otherwise, I could at least ask what in all the worlds Alice was doing, because that hard thing was poking at my lips again. A jolt of panic zapped through me when I thought she might be trying to pry my mouth open to get a look at my fangs. I wouldn't have put that past her, not since the reason we'd become friends was because of her curiosity. She was worse than a cat, so maybe that was why her and Dominic butted heads all the time. The thought nearly made me smile.

All thought evaporated from my mind when my lips were parted, whatever hard thing Alice was sticking in my mouth slipping in. Warm liquid filled my mouth next, and I wanted to gag and choke so I could spit it out, but some of it went down my throat and that was all it took. I gulped it greedily, going as far as sucking on what had to be a straw to get more of it. With each swallow I felt more alive, the tingling feeling intensifying through my body. After a few moments of drinking, I managed to unglue one eyelid and squint at the room I was in.

Alice's face popped above me, and seeing her huge eyes through the glasses she wore had me choking.

"See? It worked." Smirking like she just discovered the Americas, she looked up at, I guessed, Dominic over my head. "Now what are you going to say?"

Unwilling to release the blood, I kept sucking on the straw as if my life depended on it, moving my head slightly up to look at now-grumbling shifter. His face came into view upside down, but seeing the worry etched on his face tightened my throat. Deep lines slashed his forehead and dark circles made smudges under his green eyes. I was about to pull the straw out when Alice stabbed a finger at his face, shouting "A ha! I was right." A red rope dangled from her arm, and for some reason I reached for it. She saw me move and slapped my hand away with a scowl.

"Don't touch that. It took me forever to find a vein." This time I did choke, and I sputtered all the blood in my mouth over my chin and face. "Hey, that's not nice to spit out what was given as a gift."

Yanking the straw—which wasn't a straw at all—out of my mouth, I coughed up a lung before I traced the tube from her inner elbow to the end I was holding in my hand. "What the hell are you doing, Alice?" I rasped, my throat raw and burning from each word as if I'd been screaming for days.

"She's feeding you," Dominic deadpanned, folding his arms across his chest. "I told her to wait until you awaken, but your human is more stubborn than you."

"She's not my human."

"I'm not an object."

We both spoke over each other, and the biggest shock of my life happened when Dominic threw his head back and released a deep belly laugh. His face was turned up, and his chest shook from the guffawing. Tears gathered at the corners of his closed eyes. Alice and I naturally gawked like brainless idiots.

"Well it worked, thank you very much." Alice recovered first, clearing her throat and pushing her glasses up her nose. "Did you see how she was sucking on that tube like a baby goat on a tit? Not a vampire, my ass."

"You were right, human." Small chuckles and snickering still escaped his full lips, but he thumped his chest a couple of times and fought to control the expression on his face. "I concur."

"Did you get Johnathan?" The memory of the fight pushed any humor away, so I threw my legs to the side of the couch and sat up. Bile burned the back of my throat when his words floated through my mind.

"That was your friend?" When I just glared at Dominic for daring to use the word friend in the same context as that asshole, he lifted both his palms up in surrender. "I just wanted to know if it's the same male, that's all. And no, he was long gone when I went looking for him."

"You shouldn't have let him escape." Panting through the panic that Johnathan was now in front of the Council spilling his guts and gloating that he could still snitch on me, I gripped the edge of the couch hard enough I heard the fabric rip under my fingers. Another thought hit me, and my gaze shot to Dominic's. "The dagger. I think I dropped it at the front of the house."

"In the kitchen." His chin pointed at the closed door leading to the kitchen that Alice was opening,, the tube still attached to her elbow and the other end held up with her finger pressed over the opening.

"I cleaned it too, Brooklyn. My dad used to collect them, so I learned how to do that when I was younger." Her voice came muffled through the walls, but I was focused on the wolf curled up in a ball in front of the fireplace, his front leg and tail wrapped in gauze. And of course he was glaring at me.

"What happened to him?" Dominic glanced at the wolf, and when he met my gaze again, mirth danced in his eyes.

"He got scratched playing with the big boys in the forest, but the human acted like his intestines were spilling out." Chuckling under his breath, he kept his voice low so Alice didn't hear him. "She fussed over him as much as she did over you. Consider yourself lucky there was only enough of that fabric for him or you would've woken up as a mummy."

I tried.

I really didn't want to laugh, but it bubbled out of me in waves until a stitch in my side where I was stabbed took my breath away. I couldn't have been asleep for long if it was still healing. Dominic was next to me in the blink of an eye, lifting my chin with a crooked finger under it.

"What's wrong?" He searched my face, but I was stunned mute and couldn't answer him. "What do you feel?"

"It's nothing." I had to clear my throat twice so I could speak. "Just a reminder that if you let a sharp blade near you, it'll hurt. That's all."

"They didn't carry just blades." He still held my face up to his, a line forming between his brows. "Those were spelled to make you bleed out."

Pulling out of his grip, I leaned back on the couch and yanked my shirt up to see the stab wound. My skin was red where the sword glided in, but there was nothing else wrong with it. I wasn't still bleeding, which is what I would expect if what Dominic said was true. When my eyes found his in question, a blush crept across his stubbled cheeks. My jaw dropped at that. Clearing his own throat, he moved away, shuffling his feet uncomfortably and looking at everything but me.

"When the human couldn't stop the bleeding I … I gave you some of my blood." I could barely breathe, so I just stared at him. "I didn't know if it would help, but I had to try. You were going to die if I didn't." We both knew that was a lie, but we both ignored it.

I wouldn't have woken up, and I'd be in an internal sleep if I bled out, but the moment blood reached me I'd be up like I'd had a good night's sleep. Something else was nagging at me more than that, though, so I blurted it out without thinking.

"She didn't know if the tube would work. That's why she tried it on herself."

My gaze dropped to his left wrist, which he was pressing on the side of his leg, as I asked. He wasn't fast enough to hide one of the red dots—a mark from my fangs. A shifter would never willingly offer blood to one of my kind. They'd rather die than let us have a drop of it. I was lucky that I was sitting, because surely I was about to faint. The rushing of blood was like a train in my ears.

"I owed you that for standing up to your kind." His attitude changed and the shifter I'd met the first time I saw him returned. "Don't you dare think you'll get one more drop again."

Still mute, I watched him storm out of the house and slam the front door behind him. I searched within myself to see if I felt any different but i found nothing. Only then did I release a shuddering breath, my mind a whirl of confused thoughts. Having his blood might change things inside me but it may take time. Unable to deal with all of it at once I pushed that worry aside, I'll deal with it if the need arises. This was all surreal. It could've been the injury still messing me up. Or maybe I did die and this was some personal hell or something.

Alice came back and broke me out of that rabbit hole. She moved around the living room, her hair bouncing around with her rushed steps. Head spinning from Dominic's confession, I followed her silently with my eyes. I didn't know what to think. So, when Alice came behind me and started waving her hands over my head, I swatted at her while ducking to avoid being smacked.

"What are you doing, Alice?" Wincing when the injury

sent another pain shooting through my side, I narrowed my gaze at her.

"I'm trying to clear your aura." Showing me a clear stone clutched in her hand, the human frowned at me as if I was a disobedient child. "Dominic said you should've died, and I see you believe in energy and crystals, so what's the problem, Brooklyn? I know what I'm doing."

"I believe in what now?" Distracted by her comment, it took a second to see her waving that clear stone over my head again. I slapped her hand, which sent it flying to the side. "Stop that. What do I believe in?"

"Energy and crystals." She pointed at all the bracelets clinking on her wrists before turning one damning finger at my throat. "You are wearing a blood stone. So what's the problem? I don't understand. It'll make you feel better."

"You know what this is?" Pulling the chain up and letting the pendant dangle, I searched her face.

"I told you it's a blood stone." Pushing the thick frames up her nose, she leaned forward to see it better. "This one has been carved with symbols, but yeah, it's one. I'd recognize it anywhere. Those look like sigils," she murmured the last part under her nose.

My heartbeat sped up at this information. If what she said was true, for the first time I had a starting point, somewhere to begin looking for a way of removing it. And, if by some chance the human had any power inside her that I couldn't detect, Alice just might be the answer to a lot of my prayers. Still focused on Alice's face, I took a deep breath.

"Dominic." I didn't have to shout because I felt his agitated presence on the porch.

The door opened and the shifter walked in, his once again distrustful gaze locking on mine.

"Alice knows what the stone of the pendant is." I didn't

look away as the wariness on his face was replaced by excitement.

"Why is it such a big deal?" Alice huffed. "You two are acting like I'm a monkey that figured out how to fit the right shapes in a slot."

"Do you think you can find out what the symbols are?" Afraid to hope too much, I kept my voice even.

"I can do better than that," she told me proudly. "I have an entire encyclopedia on sigils. I'll be right back."

"I'll be damned." Dominic whistled, rubbing the back of his neck. "You were right. The human is more useful than she looks, I'll give you that."

"Yes." Dropping the pendant, I allowed hope to bloom in my chest for the first time in a long time. "Yes, she is."

Chapter Sixteen

At first Alice would harshly tilt my chin out of her way to bring her face as close as she could to the pendant, comparing the engraved swirls to every second page she turned in the thick book opened on her lap. When I pointed out she didn't have to be that close, I was informed she wasn't a vampire like me and she wouldn't chew on my throat, much to Dominic's amusement. The shifter was back to his new persona, smiling and bickering with the human back and forth like they'd known each other for years. I, on the other hand, wondered who Dominic really was. It was like two people sharing the same mouthwatering body, and that left me confused as hell.

So, when Alice suggested he should trace the symbols on a piece of paper and she tore a blank page from old note-book, I had to gulp my panic down. I also had to breathe through my mouth the entire time his face was so close to mine because I felt every breath passing his lips. While he was focusing on the pendant, I used the opportunity to study him. His square jaw was still covered in stubble that he absentmindedly scratched with a rasp of his fingers, while a slight frown pulled his eyebrows over his eyes. He was making sure every line was drawn correctly, and his eyes flicked back and forth constantly as he traced the design on the paper with a steady hand.

His upper lip was little thinner than the lower one, which curled outward and formed a shadow at the top of his chin. The corners of his eyes were slightly tilted up, and the reddish tint to his skin made him so different than me that my fingers twitched from the need to touch him. Of course I curled them tightly into fists and stuck them under my thighs in case they acted on their own when I wasn't paying attention. A movement behind him made me look over his head and panic shot through me. Alice was standing up grinning like a fool and giving me a thumbs up.

"Don't move," Dominic murmured, his deep voice sending a shiver through me.

Pressing my lips in a thin line from displeasure, I jerked my head to the side to tell her to stop her pantomime before he saw her. Wasn't she sitting next to me staring at her damn book? Being around the human was like I would've imagined babysitting a child would be like. The second my eyes were off her she caused some sort of trouble. This was proved when Dominic turned to look over his shoulder and caught her with her hands folded at the center of her chest and batting her eyelashes at me. I was sure at that point that I did die and that this was my hell.

'Oh, carry on, Dominic." Not missing a beat, she shuffled closer and leaned over both of us. "I'm just admiring your skill. Your hand is so steady. I would've messed it up by now."

He grunted something I didn't understand but turned back to his task. I was going to strangle her the second the shifter was done. To make matters worse, she petted him on the shoulder like she did to one of her animals, which made him growl deep in his chest.

"Alice." Saying her name as a warning did exactly nothing.

"Fine, geez. A girl can't do anything right around the two of you." Prancing a few steps, she plopped on the couch next to me and fanned out the skirt of the dress she wore. "I'm trying to lighten the mood," she continued, unperturbed by my glare. "That one jerk that escaped might tell the rest where we are. And then they'll find us again. We could die tomorrow for all we know. Might as well enjoy life." With a shrug of her shoulder, she pushed her ever-sliding glasses up and picked up her book.

"They already know where we are." Not wanting to give her false hope that we were safe, I told her the truth. "More will come at nightfall tomorrow just like every night so far."

Dawn was approaching fast. I could feel it in my bones. My breathing was slowing, and my movements were becoming sluggish and delayed. Through the window the sky was changing from deep gray to faded pinkish and purple shades. It pulled at the center of my chest to bring me under so I could rest. I fought it with everything in me.

"What do you mean they'll come again tomorrow just like every night?" Confused, Alice looked from me to Dominic, who was finding the pendant even more fascinating now. "I thought we were good now since we've had no trouble for two days."

I tried to jump to my feet, but Dominic placed one warm hand on my thigh and froze me in place. The heat that radiated from it burned my skin, though not in a painful way. It was in the most inappropriate way, and it sent butterflies fluttering through my belly. My thighs tensed in reaction, and he snatched his hand back with a frown on his face, staring at it like it belonged to someone else.

"How long was I asleep healing?" No amount of breathing could hide the slight tremble in my voice.

"Two days and almost two nights," Dominic answered while glaring at his now-clenched fist.

It should've been the first thing I asked, but that wasn't important anymore. I knew how the Syndicate operated. There was no way they'd left us alone for that long. My gaze found Dominic's face again, but this time I stared at it in a new light. The smudges under his eyes shouldn't have been that noticeable, and there were lines of strain etched on his handsome face that twisted my stomach in knots. There was no doubt left in my mind that he hadn't slept all that time.

"They did come." Not looking away from the top of his head, I waited. "I took care of it," was all he offered before picking up the pencil again and returning to what he was doing.

I didn't know what to say. He not only protected Alice, but he kept me safe while I couldn't defend myself, too. It would've been so easy to just walk away, or even to take the human and hide her somewhere safe while leaving me to my fate when the Syndicate found me. I would've bet my life that was what he would've done the first time I woke up in his small apartment. Now?

Now I had no idea what to think.

"Thank you." His head jerked up and his gaze locked on mine at my whispered gratitude.

"You would've done the same." Dominic spoke those words, but his eyes searched the truth on my face.

My lips parted but nothing came out of them. Everything around us faded into nothingness until I was left snared in his eyes like a deer stuck in a steel trap. Something strange and foreign passed between us in that moment. I could almost physically feel it twining and tugging me toward him. He must've felt it too, because he leaned closer just as I did, our faces left separated only by a breath. My heart hammered against my breastbone, all signs of the approaching dawn forgotten when he dropped the pencil and his hand glided up my shin to my thigh. If he held a dagger in his other hand intending to stab me, I would've let him just so I didn't look away from his eyes.

"They were here and you didn't tell me?" Alice screeched, her words breaking the moment.

"I took care of it," Dominic replied much more harshly than before, and I shook my head to clear it. What the hell just happened? "There was no need to frighten you," he added to soften the impact of his earlier snarl.

"Okay, here is the deal." Agitated, Alice started flipping through the book in such a way I thought she would rip the pages. "My house, my rules. From now on, I want to know who comes and who goes, understood?" When she turned to see us both gaping at her, she nodded once sharply as if she'd made her point. "I'd rather know if someone is coming to chew on my neck than them coming out of nowhere. As you both like to remind me every second, I'm human. Surprise attacks are all I have going for me. I can't surprise shit if I don't know it's coming."

Dominic's mouth opened and closed a few times before he lifted himself off the floor where he was sitting at my feet, making a shadow fall over me from his impressive height. Alice and I both craned our necks to look at his face, which was devoid of emotions. Unsure of what he was planning to do, I tensed, ready to jump up and stop him if he tried to throttle the human. I wouldn't have blamed him because I wanted to do it too, but I would've stopped him, nonetheless.

"She is your human," Dominic repeated the statement he made a few days ago before turning on his heel and walking out of the house, closing the front door softly behind him with a click.

"He knows I'm not a pet, right?" Alice muttered in annoyance.

My eyes flicked to the wolf sleeping in front of the fireplace and one of his eyes popped open to stare at me. My raised eyebrow did nothing but made that one eye narrow in a challenge. I might not want to hurt Alice, but that asshole was fair game if he didn't stop whatever game he was playing.

"Yes, he knows," I answered her, but I couldn't stop the chuckle when I saw her frowning face. "But you must understand that no one dares to talk to us the way you do."

"Oh, I'm sorry your majesties." Exaggerating the words, she rolled her eyes at me. It only made my grin grow.

"He will get used to it; he just needs time." Snickering under my breath when I heard the growl coming from the porch, I reached out for the first time to touch her without reason. With a reassuring squeeze to her hand—and being careful not to crush her fragile human bones—I smiled. "Thank you for taking care of me." My throat closed up tight.

No one but Veronica had done something like that. Now not just Alice, but Dominic as well, went out of their way to care for me, and it was too overwhelming to grasp all at once. Some of the emotions I was trying to suppress must've shown, because the next thing I knew, Alice was wrapped around me like a boa, her arms squeezing as tight as she could.

"You are welcome, Brooklyn. If you take away the whole chewing on the neck part, you are actually a very nice person." Pulling away, she didn't let go of me. "You don't smile much, which is a shame, but all things considered, I wouldn't smile either if I lived around all those grumpy, snarly jerks."

"You might have a point there, human." Snorting, I patted her awkwardly on the back, though I didn't know what to do with my hands.

Alice noticed and, removing one of her hands from my upper arm, she took hold of my limbs to wrap them around her shoulders before returning to hug me tight. I had to blink fast to get rid of the burn that started at the back of my eyes, and that was when Dominic opened the front door. Our eyes locked and he just stood there watching me with that same weird expression I'd seen on his face a few times before. I was the first to drop my gaze, embarrassment warming my cheeks because I was showing weakness in front of him. He cleared his throat and the lines on his face softened, but Alice once again cut whatever he was about to say.

"Brooklyn, we found it." I winced when she shrieked close to my ear. "Look!"

Wiggling out of my hold, she dropped to her knees and snatched the still-unfinished design Dominic was drawing, bringing it to the open page of the book. There were still a few lines left for the sketch to be done, but there was no mistaking that the symbol was exactly the same. Holding my breath, I leaned over the couch to get closer too, sensing, more than hearing, Dominic join us. All three of us stared at the picture without saying a word for a long moment. Until Alice broke the tense silence and asked the one question that was no doubt on all of our minds.

"Why on earth would anyone carve a binding sigil on your pendant, Brooklyn?"

"Yeah, why indeed," I muttered under my breath, still staring at the page.

"I think I might have an idea why." Dominic shocked me, but whatever he was about to say couldn't be good judging by the look on his face.

Another shitstorm coming, my mind announced.

Chapter Seventeen

"Well?" Alice snapped after the shifter kept staring at me without saying anything. "Are you going to tell us or should we start guessing here?"

"It has something to do with you being different than the rest of your kind." Dominic's deep voice had the most inappropriate effect on me at the worst of times.

All that aside, hearing I was different over and over my whole life, well, it started to grate on my nerves after a while. It wasn't his fault for phrasing it that way, but I couldn't stop the grimace from lining my mouth when I heard it. "Of course it's because I'm different." I piped in sardonically.

Ignoring my comment, he focused on the pendant, talking to it instead of me. "After you got injured, I went back out to retrieve the dagger I knew must've fallen where you fought. I wasn't aware the steel was mixed with silver until I picked it up and it almost melted the skin of my hand. That's when I saw the spell around it, and then I got to thinking."

"This is like watching *The Originals* live," Alice gushed, lifting her knees to her chest and hugging them with a firm push of her glasses up her nose.

We both ignored her.

"When the second attack came, I kept one of them alive so I could try to remove the pendant." Dominic continued eyeing Alice through narrowed lids as if daring her to interrupt him. She grinned but stayed quiet, thankfully. "Call it curiosity if you will, or distrust, but I thought you were doing something to prevent me from taking it off you when I tried."

"Of course you did," I murmured acerbically, which earned me the same look as the one the human got.

"It came off without any resistance."

I blinked at him. "I'm sorry?"

"I ripped it off his throat with little effort."

"It can't be. It doesn't come off." Tension started at the center of my forehead, though it was probably caused by my intense frown.

"Have you tried taking a pendant off of someone else?" the shifter asked slyly, and that had me scowling at him.

"No, I haven't. Why would I?"

"Exactly my point. Back inside, I tried taking yours off again. It wouldn't budge unless I cut your head off. Theirs come off, yours doesn't. It has something to do with ..." he struggled for a word, so I saved him from the misery.

"Me being different, yes we heard." That had the opposite effect from the one I was expecting. The lines on Dominic's face softened and he filled his chest to bursting before blowing out a sigh.

"Different is not necessarily a bad thing, Brooklyn. Not from where I'm standing." That time when he said my name there was so much weight placed behind it that my heart skipped a beat before drumming against my chest.

"To me it has always been a hindrance, so I wouldn't know." Scrubbing a hand over my face, I looked at the open page next to me. "There is no way we can find a witch willing to undo whatever was done. The only witches I've seen belong to the Syndicate."

Somewhere along the way the idea of having the pendant removed had become important to me. It could've been when I saw Veronica rip hers off, because to me it seemed like that set her free, and I wanted that freedom, though I knew I'd never have it. Or maybe it happened after seeing Dominic's disgust when he looked at it. One way or another, it was just another thing that I could use to flip the Council off, so I was all for it.

"Hello." Alice waved her hand in front of my face, her eyes as wide as saucers behind her thick glasses. "Witch right here, didn't you hear what I said before we left my kennel?"

"Alice"—On a sigh, I watched her, my mind racing to come up with how to say something without offending her. "The witch we need might mean something different to humans. I don't sense that power in you."

"Oh, that's fine." Acting like I just told her she is the master witch of the universe, she grinned and jumped to her feet. Her glasses tilted sideways on her face, but she didn't seem to notice. "That's because I'm not ready. First, I have to open a circle. It's how this works. Trust me, Brooklyn. I'll be right back."

Dominic and I watched her dart out of the living room and disappear into the kitchen, then a few seconds later pots and pans started banging, the loud noises followed by the crash of a glass breaking. Both of us flinched from the sound and turned to glance at each other.

"I don't have the heart to tell her in any different way." Confessing under my breath, I looked away from him.

"No harm in trying. What do we have to lose?"

"Time?"

"We have nothing but time until nightfall." Turning away from me, Dominic walked up to the window, folding his hands at the small of his back. His wide shoulders obscured almost the entire thing, the lightening sky casting a bright glow like an aura around his body.

"We were also different." His deep voice had a faraway quality as if he was talking to himself, not me. "My family and I."

A steel band tightened around my chest and prevented me from taking a full breath when I heard that. I felt so alone and lost even with Veronica filling a small void in my life, and I never knew my family. How much harder would it had been if, like Dominic, I had them until the Syndicate took them away forever? In honor of his loss, I stayed silent, knowing full well the burden of his loss was partly on my shoulders too. I was guilty by association, but guilty, nonetheless.

"I had two sisters and a brother." Dominic stunned me by continuing his story. More guilt churned like acid in my stomach for the feeling of relief washing over me when I heard he wasn't talking about a mate. "All of us, including my parents, were different than any other shifter we knew. We were faster, stronger … Alphas of packs and tribes kneeled the moment they were close enough to feel our power."

I flinched when the banging in the kitchen started again because I was so intent on hearing everything he was saying.

It was almost like I was in a trance from the sound of his voice.

"We could partly shift, too."

He turned to look at me over his shoulder at that, and I couldn't control the widening of my eyes. I've heard of partial shifts, but I thought that was also a myth. *Just like the myth of your talent for compulsion.* The voice in my head didn't skip a beat. Realizing my mouth was parted, I closed it and bit the inside of my cheek because I looked like a fool.

"I guess that was forbidden." A sad smile curled his lips when his gaze flicked across mine. "No one warned us of that."

"I'm sorry." The useless apology was just a breath leaving my lips, but he nodded twice before facing the window again.

"They were all terrified of the Syndicate, so when we moved here shifters started coming in flocks. At first my father was happy to give them a safe place to stay, but after a while he realized they had no intention of leaving."

"So your family left?" My question elicited a humorless laugh from him.

"We purchased a larger piece of land and we built a compound. A sanctuary, he liked to call it." The shake of his head was like a razor cutting through my heart. "We were fools. Thinking just because our family was different and since we now had numbers that we stood a chance."

It took effort to swallow the lump in my throat.

"They attacked in waves, witches spread among them like seeds." His hands fisted into a white-knuckled grip. "We stood no chance at all. All those coming for safety didn't even try to fight. They stood there being slaughtered like cattle. We couldn't believe what we were seeing. Pride killed my family as much as the Syndicate did. My father refused to stand down or run, while those who trusted him to protect them died. So, he told my sisters, my mother, and my brother to attack, and he followed right behind them."

"And you?" The hot tears rolling down my face made my voice crack, but I didn't care at that point.

I could see from the stiffness of his shoulders and by the tone of his voice that he wanted to cry. He was crying inside but wouldn't let a tear betray him. He accused his family of being prideful, but pride held him together now, though I could hear the broken pieces in him grind together. So, I cried for him. Shamelessly, letting the tears trickle down my cheeks and soak into my shirt.

"I was the youngest of my siblings, so I was left behind to hide, to protect our lineage, in case the worst happened." he spat with so much venom my spine snapped straight and I was so alert it was as if I'd been zapped by a thousand watts. "They all died that night. When I finally was brave enough to step out in the open, I walked through a sea of headless corpses arranged like some macabre celebration in the middle of the field. My father was positioned at its head, his body placed on a pike to keep his spine straight. My mother was at his feet, along with my sisters, but I never found my brother's body." He cleared his throat, rolling his shoulders. "I'm sure it was between the hundreds sprinkled on the grass. I couldn't find the strength to go search, but I promised them all their deaths would not be in vain. I swore on my honor, the coward that I was, that I would hunt the Syndicate one by one until none of them remain."

Dominic turned to face me, and his features were set in granite, but his green eyes were glossy until he blinked his pain away. At seeing my teary face, he paused, his gaze darting to the damn pendant on my throat before locking back on mine. I clenched my hands so I didn't grab the chain and yank it off right along with my head if need be. I'd been bitter and angry, but I'd never until that very moment been ashamed of what I was. He must've read it on my face because he lowered his chin, more of a short bow of acknowledgment than a nod, and he shuffled his feet uncomfortably.

"I might be making the biggest mistake I've ever made after staying hidden that night, but I told you all this so you know that I have every intention of keeping my word. I will kill every single one of you that is part of the Syndicate."

My lips parted and I was ready to bare my neck and let him start with me. There was no doubt in my mind he would kill us all, and by doing so he would avenge Veronica's death too. My life for everything the Syndicate had taken from him was too small of a sacrifice, but it was the only one I had, and I was willing to offer it. Just like with everything he had said until now, he shocked me again.

"That is why I want you to take that pendant off." That explained why he was fidgety all of a sudden. "As I said, it might be my biggest mistake, but you ..." Cocking his head to the side, he made my heart skip a beat when his panther stared at me through the glowing irises. "You, Brooklyn, are different. In the predicament we find ourselves, that's definitely not a bad thing."

Not knowing what to say to that, I just sat there silent and held my breath when he walked up to me and kneeled in front of my knees so that we were at eye level. His hand lifted to my face to cup my cheek, and his thumb rasped across my skin when he tried wiping the never-ending tears away. Where our skin touched, tingles spread over me and tickled my throat. The couch was firm enough to be steady, but I felt like the whole house was swaying from his nearness and the look in his eyes. No one had ever looked at me that way, and my whole existence reacted as if coming out of a deep sleep. Dominic's lips inched closer to mine and I was trapped in his gaze.

"Oh my God, that was so romantic," Alice squealed, clapping her hands from the door of the kitchen, and we both jumped away as if we'd been burned. "Hey! No, no, no. You need to kiss her now, man. Don't be a cock tease."

Covering my face with both hands, I wished I didn't start caring about the human as much as I did. In the true fashion prescribed to my kind, I really wanted to rip her throat out that second. Every step that Dominic took away from me left me cold, and my chest felt hollow. Was he really going to kiss me? Did he really mean what he'd said about my pendant? Did I finally make him see me, Brooklyn, instead of a pawn of the Syndicate? I was too afraid to hope, so I shoved those thoughts away in the deep recesses of my mind next to Veronica's death so I could deal with them later. Or never.

Never sounded like a wonderful plan, actually.

"Anyway"—Alice looked sheepish when I peeked at her through my fingers, her cheeks burning bright red—"I'm ready to do magic." Wiggling her fingers, she giggled nervously.

Dominic groaned.

Closing my eyes, so did I.

Chapter Eighteen

"The human is aware that you are not a demon, correct?" Dominic muttered next to me, his head titled toward me so she didn't hear us. "That looks like something for a demon to me."

Too aware of his nearness, I struggled to maintain my focus on what Alice was doing. She made Dominic push the furniture next to the walls so the center of the small room was clear. I was entrusted only with the rolling of the rug because I was still hurting from my injury. Her words, not mine, and since I didn't want her wrapping me up like the wolf still sleeping like the dead in the corner, I obeyed. She made us stand at the window so we didn't get in her way, and we watched her pour salt on floor for twenty minutes before she waved a butcher knife in the air, brandishing it like a sword. She was calling the elements, according to her at least. My gaze bounced off the picture frames covering the walls, and I had a feeling her parents were laughing at us while watching this the whole charade, too.

A pentagram was also drawn in salt at the center of

the circle with tealight candles placed at its points, the flames flickering from the breeze her movements created. With the book clutched to her chest, Alice walked barefoot around while muttering nonsense, pausing once in a while to push her thick glasses up her nose. I should've put an end to the insanity, but one look at her twinkling eyes and exited face clamped my mouth shut as if sealed closed.

"I'm pretty sure it's for a demon," Dominic continued, and my lips twitched at the corners.

"She insists on calling me a vampire. Humans think that vampires are soulless monsters, no? That's the same as a demon." My lips barely moved, but Dominic chuckled at that.

"At least we are being entertained." His deep voice rumbled in his chest, and it raised goosebumps on my arms.

"I've been thinking." I changed the subject because the longer he kept smiling and acting the way he was, the more difficult it was for me to keep my distance.

"And before you deny it, be aware that I remember some things from the night Veronica was killed." I could feel his eyes burning a hole into the side of my face, but I kept my gaze on Alice as she moved around, this time with a bird feather in her hand. "You have an informant in the Syndicate. I heard him tell you to get me out of there."

"I do." He was watching me intently, his voice giving nothing away.

"Is it Samir?"

"What difference does it make?" He shifted slightly and his shoulder made contact with mine, the touch sending a current through my spine. "When they lose their usefulness, they are going to die, too."

"Fair enough." I nodded once to show him the respect I

had for his statement. "But I think I have a plan on how to cut a big hole in their impenetrable shield."

We both flinched when Alice flicked water from a cup in our direction, and our reaction made the human grin like a fool. Unable to stop myself, I snickered, at least until I noticed that Dominic stared at me with parted lips. A blush crept up my cheeks and I ducked my head to hide it.

"Do tell," he prompted after clearing his throat.

"We expect them to attack tonight, right?"

"Like every night, yes."

"What if we are not here when they arrive?"

"You are still not fully healed, and the human has a shed full of animals. Where do you plan on taking them all?"

"To pay the Council a visit." I turned to face him as I said it, and his eyebrows shot all the way to his hairline. "After a few attacks that haven't gone their way, the Council will send most of the guards tonight. They are going to flatten this place to the ground with or without us here."

"And you know this how?"

"I've seen it happen way too many times." I didn't look away when his eyes narrowed, the thick lashes framing them casting shadows over his high cheekbones. "A small number will be left to guard them, but they are arrogant enough to think neither you or I will dare go to them now that they are hunting us."

"What if they expect it? The three of them are aware that you know the way they operate." Folding his arms across his chest, he leaned heavily on the wall. "No, it could be a trap."

"There or here, we will die tonight either way." His head snapped my way. "They've already scouted this place enough by now to know everything there is about it. All its weaknesses. Us going there will at least give us a slight chance."

"You are asking me to trust you." It wasn't said in accusation, but he did look at the pendant when he said that.

"Yes." Butterflies erupted in my stomach and my ears buzzed from the rushing of the blood in my veins. "Yes, I'm asking you to trust me."

He was silent for a long time, and it looked like Alice was nearing the end of whatever it was that she was doing, so I was certain he wasn't going to answer. So when he spoke, my body gave a jolt as a reaction to the unexpected sound. It made him grin, the carefree smile giving him a boyish look.

"Very well, Brooklyn." Cracking his neck, he turned to watch Alice do her finishing touches. "Let us do this your way, but remember one thing: just because I said that I want the pendant off your neck so you can live and I can still keep my oath, it doesn't mean I won't do it."

"I wouldn't dream of it," I told him dryly.

"Okay guys, I think I'm ready," Alice announced, waving us to approach her. "Come stand at the center of the pentagram, Brooklyn, just don't step on the salt. You, Dominic, stand on the outside of the circle close to me so you can go take the pendant off when I'm done."

Dominic and I begrudgingly shuffled to take our positions, Alice watching where we were placing our feet like a hawk. When I tried to pass her, she touched my forearm to get my attention, which made me look at her face.

"Was he flirting with you?" Human whispering was like talking in a normal tone of voice to supernatural ears. Dominic heard her as clearly as I did.

"Yeah." Glancing at him, I stepped over the circle and ignored the flipping of my belly from his look. "He was flirting." I spoke louder, smiling sadly at her excited face. "Now what?"

"Okay, I'm going to draw the sigil in the air in front of your face with each object representing the elements, and after that we will pour salt water over it." Adjusting her glasses, she peeked at the open book at her feet. "According to the book, if the sigil is used for binding without knowledge or agreement from the bound person, the salt water, with the help of the elements, will negate its effect."

"I take my words back." Dominic snickered. "She doesn't think you are a demon. The human thinks you are possessed."

"Are you a witch, Mr. smartass?" Both hands on her hips, Alice squared off with the shifter." I didn't think so. Stay quiet and just rip the pendant off when it's time." Squinting for a second, she changed her mind. "No, don't rip it off, you act unstable and you might rip her head off along with it. Just tug on it gently, okay muscles?"

Seeing the incredulous look on Dominic's face was priceless, and my nostrils flared while I tried to hold back my laughter. Lips twitching and jaw working, I managed, but not before he saw it and gave me a deep scowl. I was sure I would've failed controlling my reaction soon enough, but luckily Alice started waving things at me and I focused back on her.

The human shouted for each element to come aid her and wiggled the feather, the clear stone, and a cup of water in my face. She went as far as spraying my face by flicking her fingers, much to Dominic's amusement. A tick developed in my jaw the more animated she became, yet I couldn't feel an ounce of power coming from her or the circle she made. So when she snatched the butcher's knife and began brandishing it too close for my liking, I decided it was time to put a stop to the charade. It was one thing to humor her so I didn't make her feel bad, and totally another if she could injure herself or me. Just because it wouldn't kill me didn't mean it wouldn't hurt like a bitch.

Tracking her hand, I waited and tried to time it right so I could grab her wrist. She was so engrossed in what she was doing that if half the Syndicate walked in right then Alice wouldn't have noticed. Unfortunately, as I stepped out and reached to take the knife from her, her eyes locked on mine before widening and she slashed the hand holding the knife down in an arch. The blade cut deep across my outstretched arm, the burn from it clenching my jaw tight. Dominic snarled from the side, but thankfully he didn't move from his place outside the salt circle. I didn't want Alice hurt. I, on the other hand, would heal in a matter of seconds.

The strength of her jerky movement pitched her body to the side, and I circled her shoulders to prevent her from falling. That placed me right on the inside edge of the circle so my blood trickled on top of the salt. It sizzled like pouring water over boiling oil, and everywhere it touched the salt sparks spit across the floor. A blinding light flung me back and forced me to release Alice. I ended up thrown at the center of the pentagram on my ass with a grunt.

"Brooklyn!" Dominic's roar made my ears ring for a few moments while I blinked fast to get rid of the blindness. "Brooklyn!"

But I couldn't answer him. Power erupted all around me, snapping shut like an invisible lid placed over the salt circle. It was so strong my skin felt like it was melting off my bones. Reaching out blindly, I patted the floor and fumbled to my knees in the hopes I could find a way out. The pain was preventing me from answering the shifter, and my teeth were glued together in a soundless snarl. *Oh, dear fates, Alice.* Panic gripped me like a vice and I found my will to speak.

"Alice." Croaking through a raw throat, I crawled slowly forward. "Dominic, check on Alice." I could've sworn I heard him growl *stubborn female*, but my ears were still ringing so I wasn't sure. "Is she alive?" Surely that much power could kill a human.

"She's unconscious, but alive," Dominic spat angrily after I heard him stomp around the circle. "If it was up to me, I'd kill her myself for this."

"It wasn't her fault." Jumping to her defense, I inched closer to his voice, my vision not clearing fast enough. The light that burst it seemed like it burned my retinas. "I shouldn't have tried to grab her like that."

"How are you doing over there?" I heard his boots thump on the floor, and I knew by the heaviness of each step that he had extra weight. He was carrying Alice to the couch was my guess.

"My vision is still blurry, and the power is unbearable, but I'll live, unfortunately." My humor was lost when he growled deep in his throat. "I'm fine," I added on a sigh.

"Well, at least we know one thing." Halfway through that his voice grew louder, which told me he'd returned to my side. "There is, indeed, a witch in the house."

"Yeah." Snorting, I rubbed the back of my hand over my eyes, and at least then I could see the blurry outline of Dominic standing as close as he could to me, the tips of his boots a hairsbreadth away from the circle. "When it comes to Alice, I've learned I can't trust my instincts. She is full of surprises."

"I wasn't talking about the human." His words were conversational, but there was no mistaking the intensity they carried.

"There was no one else doing all this demonic summoning, as you called it, or whatever it is" I reminded him, finally able to see his face. I wish I couldn't. "Who are you talking about?"

"You."

There was a flash in his green eyes that sent my heart to my feet.

Chapter Nineteen

"You have lost your mind." I had to open and close my eyes a few more times to see properly, and when I could I pushed to my feet. "You know as well as I do that I'm Atua."

"How can I ever forget that." Dominic's narrowed gaze bored into mine. "Obviously you're not just Atua."

"I'm not a hybrid," I snapped at him as if it was his fault my whole life had just turned into a disaster. "Atua can't reproduce with witches. If we could, imagine what the Council would've done with that by now."

Dominic stayed silent, but his eyes lingered on my pendant for long enough to make me fidget where I stood. Since I wasn't ready to entertain that insane idea, I chose the lesser of the two evils. Stabbing a finger at the cup of saltwater sitting next to his feet on the floor, I waited until he stopped staring at me and looked at where I was pointing.

"Might as well try and see if that will work." Muttering under my breath, I avoided his gaze, glancing at Alice on the couch and the wolf plopped in front of her protectively like a statue of a gargoyle.

After what felt like an eternity, he bent down and swiped the cup that looked like a toy in his large hand. A lock of silky hair fell over his forehead, and stupidly I envied his fingers when they stabbed through it to smooth it back. With a frown he turned it around like he'd never seen one before, bringing it first to his nose to take a whiff before handing it over. I jumped back when his hand hit the invisible barrier and saltwater sloshed all over his hand and arm. He didn't drop the cup, but it was a close call.

"You try to take it." He pushed the words through clenched teeth.

With a deep sigh, I inched my hand in his direction. To my surprise, my hand passed without a problem, only tingling when my fingers brushed against his around the cup. A shiver raced up my spine, and he noticed my reaction. A smirk tilted his lips up at one corner, and he held tighter to the cup. When my eyebrow arched, he removed his fingers one by one.

"Why do I get the feeling you are enjoying this way too much?" I drawled, moving away from him and that penetrating stare.

"Because I am." The smirk didn't magically disappear, unfortunately. "Also, it would explain many things."

"Like?" Swirling the saltwater, I watched it like it was the most fascinating thing in the world.

"The reason you are different." My gaze snapped to his and all the humor in his expression had vanished, though I didn't like what had replaced it. It made me wary. "The reason why the Council wanted you bound." He pointed at the pendant with a nod.

"By that logic, everyone in the Syndicate is a witch," I reminded him. "All of us wear the same pendant."

"Not the same, no. Just the same stone, and theirs comes off," he countered with a stubborn lift to his chin as if he was daring me to deny it. "Also, no one sent to the cages has come out and was later allowed to reintegrate back into the Syndicate's fold. Unlike you."

Dominic voiced another thing that was always scratching at the back of my mind, but I'd foolishly ignored. Having the opportunity to mess with the Council, I convinced myself that it was because of Veronica that they allowed me back in like nothing had happened. Now faced with the truth—if it was the truth—I didn't have anyone I could hide behind. The night of the fight came to mind, when the guards told me the Council had requested my presence. They were told to try and bring me in first, and if that didn't work to kill me on the spot.

Why?

"Ah, I see it's starting to make sense to you, too." Dominic nodded knowingly before folding his arms across his wide chest. The shifter was oblivious of the effect he had on people it seemed. The female population, to be more specific. "Go on, try to take it off."

It was something to do so I didn't have to think about all these new things shining in my life, so I obeyed. He startled when I had no comment or snarky remark for him but kept watch when I brought the cup closer to my chest. I expected to be annoyed by his curiosity since it was my life, after all, but I wasn't. As a matter a fact, I felt relieved that he was standing like an impenetrable wall next to me regardless that he couldn't breach the barrier.

Bracing for another blinding light, I dipped my fingers in the cup and closed my eyes before I sprayed the pendant.

The water landed more on my neck and chin than on the stone, but a few drops found their target. When no light came out, I peeked through my lashes first, unsure if there would be a delayed reaction, but nope. Nothing happened. With my heart beating on the roof of my mouth, I took hold of the chain and tugged on it. It didn't budge, but I was sure there were red welts on the back of my neck. Dominic observed me like I was a bug under a microscope, his tense shoulders relaxing when he found my eyes on him.

"According to the human, I should take it off." As soon as he was done talking, a line formed between his brows as if he was remembering he couldn't enter the circle. "That might be a little difficult."

"Now you think that Alice is the witch?" My teasing earned me a glare.

"She might not have the power of a witch, but she has the knowledge. Whatever she did activated the salt and the power of the earth in it before your blood touched it." Spreading his arms wide, he encompassed the room that Alice turned into some cult's sacrificial alter. "Not even I can deny her that acknowledgment."

He was right, of course, but I just shrugged. Some childish part of me reared its head up because I wanted nothing more than to annoy him in that moment. "Should I step out?"

"If you can, yes. Let's try that." Sliding to the side, he curled his fingers in an invitation to join him. "No, wait. Try and take me inside first. If that doesn't work, you can step out."

Wound up tight like a bow, I reached for the hand he offered with trembling fingers. For some reason, an itch started between my shoulder blades, which made me uncomfortable. The problem was it wasn't because of

Dominic. Something else was bothering me, but I couldn't figure out what. My skin burned deliciously when it connected to his, and I tugged him inside the circle. Neither of us was certain that he could pass, but he did as if nothing stood in his way. The second he stepped close enough for me to feel the heat of his body, goosebumps popped out all over my arms. I ducked my head so I didn't have to see the smirk on his face.

"Let's try now," was all he murmured before he grabbed the chain firmly.

My knees locked so I could stay in place while he yanked, though I still expected him to rip my head off along with the pendant. Dominic tugged gently at first, and I could barely feel the sliding of the metal on the back of my neck. When that didn't do anything, his palm slid around the links, stopping with the stone nestled at the center. Both of us flinched when it sizzled, and he dropped it with a feral cry. My skin pebbled for an entirely different reason this time. The predator in him warned me that he was about to attack.

"Dominic, stop." When asking nicely didn't work, I did something I never thought I would. I used compulsion. "Dominic. Stop."

He froze, the glow diminishing in his green gaze before he shook his head to clear it. I was holding my breath because I'd crossed a line I shouldn't have. If he'd been unsure about killing me up until know, I had a feeling that moment had sealed my fate. One second he was rolling his shoulders, and in the next his large palm was wrapped around my throat. He lifted me until just the tips of my boots were grazing the salt-sprinkled floor.

"Don't. You. Ever. Pull. That. Again." Each word was

snarled, each said firm enough so there was no doubt in my mind that this was an order, not a request.

"Understood." My voice was strained from the lack of oxygen my lungs were experiencing. "I didn't … I didn't want to fight you. Not now, not here."

That did it. He released me and I stumbled back a step, my hand automatically coming to rub my throat.

"No matter the circumstances, don't ever do that, Brooklyn. I'm warning you."

"You have my word." And it dawned on me what happened before I found it hard to breathe. "How did you shake it off so easily?"

"I don't know." His head tilted to the side. "It was like a fog was clouding my mind while your voice repeated the words softly, but the second adrenaline rushed through me I was able to break through it." The shifter never missed any of my reactions, so he didn't miss when my mind started racing. "What?"

"Johnathan gloated about the amulet he had to protect him from compulsion that night." When his eyebrows dipped low over his eyes, I explained my worry. "You said I couldn't heal after the stab wound, and only after you gave me your blood the skin knitted together. What if you can break out of my compulsion because I had your blood?"

"You've had Johnathan's blood?" A dark cloud loomed over his features and his expression darkened. It took me a moment to see it for what it was, and the moment I did warmth washed over me.

He was jealous.

"No." I couldn't keep the dumb smile off my face, and the scowl I received was well deserved. "He would be defanged if he tried taking mine, and I'd rather die than have a drop of his vile blood."

"I don't understand."

"When they kept me in the cages, they took my blood." Swallowing thickly, I tried speaking faster in hopes that not all the memories would return. "When I was too weak to stay awake and feel my suffering, they'd force blood down my throat, but just enough to keep me aware of what was happening. Johnathan is nothing if not cunning. If the pendant is somehow connected to me and my blood along with my gift ... well, he would've dug out that information a long time ago."

"He has that much pull in the Syndicate?"

I snorted at Dominic's question. "He is so slimy and manipulative that if you need to find any information, you should go to him. He would sell his own soul to gain an advantage." My lips pressed into a thin line and I stared at my feet. "I wish you caught him that night."

"There will be time yet," he muttered but paused when I kept twitching my shoulders. "What's wrong." My heart skipped a beat when his fingers found a loose strand that escaped my ponytail and tucked it behind my ear.

"I'm not sure." Clearing my throat, I tried controlling my breathing, but nothing was helping. "Something doesn't feel right."

"Did it work?" Alice croaked from the couch and she lifted on her elbows. "Did you take it off?"

When she saw us standing in the middle of the circle, she jumped to her feet, though she was swaying slightly. I tensed to jump and catch her if she dropped, but I shouldn't have worried. Teetering like she was drunk and pushing the wolf to the side, she stumbled toward us, both arms outstretched and her glasses barely hanging on for dear life to the tip of her nose.

"Well?" she mumbled, but her voice trailed off when the

morning light coming through the window slowly started disappearing. "What the hell is that?"

All three of us watched darkness overtake the bright blue sky, as if someone was erasing the day and replacing it with night so dark it was pitch black. The breath got stuck in my throat.

"Alice, get here," I shouted, and she didn't need to be told twice.

Before I could reach out, she bolted and dove head-first for us. The top of her head hit the invisible barrier, which sent her sprawling back like a starfish on the floor. A whimpered "Ouch" was the only sound after all the air exited her lungs with a loud whooshing grunt. Luckily her feet were close to the outside of the salt circle, so I grabbed her ankles and yanked her in with us. By this point, everything was covered in dark shadows.

"Witches," Dominic spat from above me while I crouched to check the back of Alice's head.

"What's going on? Doggy! Doggy come here." Alice shouted frantically trying to get the wolf shifter to join us, but I had no time to worry about getting him to safety too.

The entire world exploded around us.

Chapter Twenty

An inferno opened where the small house once stood, the flames licking whatever was left from the outside walls. The roof caved in raining on us, and I only had enough time to tug Alice under my body. If my bones broke, they would heal. Hers might be the end of her. The ground was rattling erratically, so I had to brace on my elbows and knees or I would've rolled away from her. Grateful when nothing dropped on top of us to crush us, I dared to glance up and see how the barrier was holding, happiness floating through me that it was strong enough to protect us.

My eyes locked on intense green ones.

Dominic was poised above me and Alice bearing the brunt of the fallen roof on his shoulders. His neck and shoulders strained, and his jaw was clenched so tight I was shocked I couldn't hear his teeth breaking. Flames were nearing his body, crawling fast up the wooden pieces and reaching for him. Panic propelled me faster than I'd ever moved before. Jumping to my feet, I took half of the roof on my own shoulders to give him a break.

"Alice, I need you to come and stand next to me." I grunted the words before shrinking into myself to stay away from the fire that looked ready to devour us. "Alice!" I snapped when she kept cowering on the floor sobbing about the dead wolf shifter and how it was her fault he died.

"Brooklyn, what is happening?" she whimpered after a while but obeyed, thankfully.

"Nothing, it's fine," I tried to reassure her. "We're fine."

But we weren't and we were not going to be. Alice knew it too, because she was looking at me like I'd lost my mind. I, on the other hand, struggled to accept the fact that Dominic was protecting me with his own body. Shifters didn't do that. Not even for their own. *Unless it's a mate or a youngling.* A voice in my mind snickered, but I shoved that stupidity away.

"The rest of the house is going to collapse any minute." Dominic's deep voice was calm as if he'd accepted our fate.

I didn't.

"They want me." His gaze narrowed, but I continued. "If I agree to go to the Council, most of them will leave to bring me to justice. "Whoever is left, you'll be able to handle on your own, just please promise me you'll take Alice with you."

"No." There was no room for argument in that one word.

"Dominic, be reasonable." Praying to whoever listened, I hoped beyond hope that he would do as I asked. "They could've killed me but sent me to the cages instead. They also kept me close after I escaped that hell. If what we were saying is true, they'll keep me alive. You'll be able to find me, but only if you are alive." I didn't know if he would want to go looking for me, but the realization that I wanted him to hit me like a battering ram.

"We will go together," he stubbornly snarled, while Alice was clutching me for dear life.

"We are surrounded. You can feel them as well as I can. Go." I hissed when flames skittered across the back of my hand that was holding the roof. "Go!"

"Stubborn female," he barked through a tight jaw. "Let go on three?" I gave him a nod and blinked back tears.

"One …"

It felt like my heart was breaking. I could literally hear it.

"Two …"

His gaze locked on mine and his face softened under all the weight he was holding.

"Th—"

"Hey guys?" Alice cut him off and yanked on my arm. I almost dropped the part of the roof I was holding on top of us both because of it. "I know how we can escape."

She was more alert, the initial shock she'd been under wearing off. Or maybe survival instincts had kicked in. One could never be sure when it came to the human. Then she spoke again and I understood what it was that made her look at Dominic and me with a fierce expression on her face.

"These fuckers killed all my animals." Her voice broke and my gut clenched. "I'll get us out of here if you promise to kill them all."

"Deal, human," Dominic answered eagerly, and he looked at her as if she was his savior. "Lead the way."

"Follow me." With a firm nod, Alice let go of me, and turning on her heel, she ducked under wooden beams, brick, and plaster avoiding the flames like a pro.

"Three!" the shifter snapped at me and moved.

I jumped away from the pressure, yanking my arms to

my chest when the large part we were holding pressed heavily on me. My shirt tightened and I was sharply tugged until my back slammed into a firm, solid chest. Arms like steel bands tightened around me, and I was spun around to face Dominic, the top of my head barely reaching his nose.

"To you, sacrificing your life might be an everyday occurrence, Brooklyn." His voice was low and so full of emotion it was choking me. "Don't you ever ask me again to agree to something like that. Understood?"

My head nodded jerkily because I was too stunned to speak.

"Hey kissy face, are we leaving or are we getting a tan in the flames first?" Alice whisper-yelled so she could be heard over the roaring fire.

"You are waiting for us, human?" I almost choked on my tongue when I heard Dominic tease her. "I thought you'd be halfway to Chicago by now."

"And leave you to get lost? Not a chance. You'll be my hitmen now, and you'll kill those fuckers one by one as soon as we get out of here." She had no idea how close she'd hit the nail with the hitman part. Not about Dominic, but me. "This way."

The salt circle was broken in multiple places, and I guessed that was the reason Alice could walk through it as if nothing was holding her out a few minutes ago. We were her shadows weaving in and out through destroyed rooms that she knew like the back of her hand. Alice was one surprise after another, and the longer I was around her, the more I learned about her. The fates must've favored me when we'd crossed paths.

"They'll wait for us to try and escape," I told Dominic, but the human heard me too, which made me frown.

"We are going down." She stabbed a finger toward her feet. "Not up."

The basement where I hid her came to mind, and a shiver clawed at my spine. I'd rather face the entire Syndicate and the raging inferno than go underground. Never again. My mind screamed in protest. Then a large hand wrapped around my icy-cold fingers, warming not just my skin but my whole inside. Glancing up, I saw Dominic looking at me over his shoulder.

"You will not be alone."

Biting on the inside of my cheek, I gave him a nod.

"Here," Alice called, pointing at a place on the floor toward the back of the house. "There is a trap door under there."

Dominic started lifting fallen pieces of the house and throwing them haphazardly wherever he could. I moved closer to help, but hearing Alice cough from all the smoke didn't sit well with me. She was helping too, dragging wooden parts with one hand while covering her mouth and nose with the other. The trap door came into view and the shifter ripped it off so he could open the fused seams. He jumped first, and after lowering Alice to him, I jumped into the dark pit.

My boots made a squelching sound as they sunk into muddy soil. The stench of moist dirt and mold was so strong my eyes watered, and I wondered if I didn't prefer the fire to the smell of a freshly dug grave. Cold swat drenched my skin and my heart was beating frantically in my throat so I kept swallowing in hopes to push it down where it belonged. I knew it'll be a long trip down this underground tunnel with my anxiety to the roof. The human was first to rush to wherever this claustrophobic place led to.

"What I want to know, human—"

"It's Alice and you know it." She spoke over him.

"...is why you have a hidden tunnel under your home," Dominic finished undeterred.

"My dad believed the government would come to break in our home and take us all to camps because they were doing DNA research to breed us with aliens," she said it all in one breath and so naturally it left us both stunned.

"Where does it lead to?" After coughing a few times, the shifter bravely continued to interrogate her.

I was done asking questions after the part about the aliens.

"Just to the outskirts of the forest close to the main road," she answered, stomping blindly through the mud, while she used her hand along one side of the dirt wall to guide us through the tunnel. "My dad's old pickup truck should still be there, too. If it has any gas left." She snorted. "I haven't checked on it in years. Who knew I'd have vampires trying to burn my house down, right?"

"You are taking this much better than I expected," I said just so I don't think about the walls closing in on me, and her laugh sounded a little unhinged.

"Oh, I'm not taking it at all, Brooklyn. I'm just pissed that my animals died." Releasing a shuddering breath, she was quiet for a moment before speaking again. "I'll go full psycho after we are out of here and safe. Oh, yeah, I'm going to lose my shit, just watch."

Dominic snickered like a boy, which was an endearing sound, but my spine stiffened like a steel pipe.

"Someone is in the tunnel with us." Snatching the shifter by the forearm, I dug my nails into his skin all my anxiety about being buried alive forgotten. "Can you feel it?" He turned this way and that, but his movements were sluggish, which sent alarms blaring through my head. "Are you hurt?"

"No."

My mouth opened to argue with him, but whoever followed us was getting too close. At that point, there was no doubt it was an Atua. Dropping the subject for later, I turned to face the way we came from just in time to see Johnathan's smug face come into view. Dominic snarled from behind me and Alice screamed.

"Keep her quiet," I muttered to the shifter as I stepped out to meet the kiss ass.

"Brooklyn, you know you can't run from me." Johnathan laughed as if we were playing some twisted game.

"Who said I was running?" Shrugging off Dominic's hand, which had tried to pull me behind him, I moved closer. "I wanted to talk with you somewhere where the rest can't overhear our conversation." Insanely, I went as far as smiling at him. "I'm glad you followed because this can't wait."

"You think me stupid?" He tsked under his breath but still kept coming, so I took a gamble, and not just with *my* life but with Alice's, too.

"The human knows ways of doing magic and discovered that I have some too." Doing my best to sound fearful, I inched closer. "Can you believe it? If the Council finds out, I'll be dead. That's why I don't want to come back, although …" Hoping my shuddering breath was believable, I ducked my chin down as if embarrassed. "It's the only home I've known."

Dominic's deadly snarl was a dagger in my chest.

"You mean it." Hearing the uncertainty in Johnathan made me want to shout in happiness, but I stared at my feet nodding. "Oh Brooklyn, you have nothing to fear, darling." My skin crawled hearing him call me that. "They've always known. It was you who was not ready to hear it yet. This is good, very good indeed. We should go back and discuss what this means for you, for us ... for the Syndicate."

"You'll help me, John?" Using the shorter version of his name like I used to when I believed we were friends sealed his fate.

"I will kill you." Dominic's deep growl from behind me made me want to cry, but I couldn't stop now that the kiss ass took the bait.

They knew. They'd always known and were keeping me alive, but for what exactly? Bile burned at the back of my throat.

"Come to me, Brooklyn." Johnathan reached for me. "I will call the others to deal with the shifter. You can have the human."

"Thank you." Whispering timidly, I rushed with my arms in front of me as if I wanted to run to his embrace.

He smiled and wrapped his arms tight around my shoulders. I lifted on my toes to be able to reach him better. Both my palms pressed on the side of his face and I twisted as hard as I could. The snapping of his spinal cord when his neck broke was the most beautiful sound I'd ever heard.

Alice screamed again.

Catching Johnathan's body in my arms, I slung him over my shoulder and turned to face Dominic. He was staring at me with an unreadable expression, but I lifted my chin up as if daring him to judge me.

"Let's go." Marching to them, I passed them both and followed the length of the tunnel. "We need to see to your injury, Dominic."

"Where do you think you are taking him?" He sneered

right on my heels, the familiar distrust from what felt like a lifetime ago back in the tone of his voice.

"With us." I shrugged with my free shoulder. "He took the bait just like I knew he would, admitting the Council knows what I am and about the magic. That means he knows a lot more than just that."

"And?" he growled.

"And he will spill every single detail he knows before I kill him. But until then, I'm planning to have fun with him."

"Good for you, Brooklyn," Alice chirped excitedly. "Girl power, man. Let her beat the fucker. He is a baddie. Damn animal killer."

"What is our next move now that we started collecting members of the Black Hand?" He begrudgingly calmed his temper, using the name for the Syndicate no one dared to say to our face.

"First we will learn everything." My heart started beating faster. "Then we will pay a visit to the Council."

And I would kill them, one by one, and with pleasure.

Dominic couldn't help but chuckle, and that sound was followed by Alice's still-a-little-disturbing laugh.

Next in the Infernal Regions for the Unprepared Series

vinci-books.com/lowerworld

The bigger the secret… the greater the body count.

On the run from the Syndicate, Brooklyn's only chance at survival lies in the truth behind her father's death. But some secrets aren't meant to be uncovered. And the Syndicate will do whatever it takes to keep Brooklyn silent—permanently.

Turn the page for a free preview…

Lower World: Chapter One

"Sooo ... do I add Mistress at the end of what I'm saying because you're a girl and I can't say Sire to you? Or do I need to say Mistress first before any other word is spoken?"

Alice leaned forward, gripping the recliner tightly on both sides of her legs while staring so intently I truly believed she was trying to use telepathy to force me to tell her the truth. I watched in fascination as the thick frames of her glasses started sliding down her nose. She's been like this ever since we did that horrible ritual to try and remove the cursed pendant that was stuck around my neck. I was desperate to have it gone at the time, unlike now when I knew better. Regardless of my feelings about it, my human friend was convinced more than ever that she was a witch and could wield magic.

I didn't agree.

There was more to Alice than met the eye—that was a fact, or she wouldn't have been able to open the circle like she did. But a witch? I'd seen the witches forced to do the

Syndicate's dirty work, and she was nothing like any of them. Nor did the cloying stench of magic I was used to smelling every time I was around a witch cling to her skin.

Tilting my head to the side, I examined her closely like I'd been doing the last few days. Ever since we managed to escape the attack from the Syndicate with our lives by the skin of our teeth. It wasn't easy running with Johnathan flung over my shoulder like a sack of potatoes while dodging Dominic's attempts of taking him so he could carry the weight. It was as endearing as it was annoying.

We found the old vehicle Alice's father had for emergencies with ease, and after a lot of praying and rattling of the rusted contraption, we left our troubles behind. Or so I hoped, anyway, at least for a while until I could think of what to do. My heart skipped a beat every time I thought about that night and what could've happened if her late father was not as paranoid as he had been before passing away. Thanks to the poor human's distrust and fascination with alien lifeforms, the three of us were alive to this day.

I'd caught Dominic looking at Alice too, but surprisingly he was being very clinical about it. Clinical *and* suspicious, and much more than necessary. Not that I wanted him to look at her with interest or anything. Just that he was a male, and Alice was a very beautiful, albeit quirky and strange, woman. The shifter's trust issues notwithstanding, nature was bound to steer his hormones in that direction. Wouldn't it?

"Well?" Alice prompted me, a line forming between her brows while she pushed the frames perched on her nose up with her forefinger. I was grateful she pulled me away from the silly thoughts swirling through my mind.

"Vampires are made up creatures the humans love to

read about, Alice. We talked about this many times. My kind are called Atua, and we do not bite humans to change them into one of us. Also, blood itself is not what sustains us; it's the lifeforce in it we need."

The sign might've been unnecessary, especially because she didn't really frustrate me with her insistence of my being a creature from fairytales. The Grimm kind of tales, if I remembered correctly, but a fictional one, nonetheless. I was just feeling the effect the daylight had on my kind down to my marrow as the early dawn slowly crept up the sky. Exhaustion tugged on my senses, and my mind was processing the exchange sluggishly. I should've slept, but I enjoyed talking to Alice too much to miss any opportunity to do so. In all the time I've known her, our exchanges were short and to the point. I did all I could to keep her away from the Syndicate's notice.

"You drink blood." The twist of her features told me she was not convinced that I was giving her the truth. "Maybe Atsua ..."

"Atua," I corrected earning myself a flat, pointed look.

"Maybe Atua," she pronounced it slowly, which I assumed was for the benefit of my addled brain. "Means vampires only in your own language. You just don't know it?" It came out as a question, and I answered only because I had a feeling she needed to talk and not think of the situation we found ourselves in. Or the dead shifter we left behind.

"What I believe is I know what I am since I've been the same being for centuries." I just couldn't help it with her, my lips twitched at the corners.

"You're making fun of me." She huffed, jerking on the recliner and crossing her arms petulantly.

I laughed.

Just a short outburst of sound, good-naturedly. She was curious by nature and obsessed with everything that wasn't human, her kennel a large statement of that. I guess I fell under the same umbrella as all her cats and dogs because she was hell bent on figuring me out. *Or she can sense if any creature is broken and she wants to heal it,* a voice in my head pointed out, and I swallowed thickly, all the humor draining from me.

"Should I lie to you and say you are right only to spare your fragile feelings?" My left eyebrow pulled on my forehead when it raised. "I will give you nothing but the truth where I can, because the only reason I would not do that is if it will put your life in danger more than it already is. I will never lie to you Alice, but I can't share everything for your safety's sake."

With lips pressed in a firm line, she just stared at me.

"You know this is the truth, do you not?"

"I don't know, Brooklyn." Flinging both her arms in the air in frustration, she groaned and buried her face in her hands. "Vampire makes sense to me. That's the reference my brain can process. You drink blood, for goodness sake. Full on chomping with those pincers like a fiend, you know what I mean?"

Words muffed through her hands, she giggled uneasily. Very slowly, her fingers spread so she could peer at me through them.

"Say something, because I feel like I'm offending you but you're being too nice to the little human with a monkey brain." Uncovering her pretty face, she gave me a sheepish look. "Please?" For a second, the smudges she left on her glasses took my attention, but I shook it off. I had to catch a couple of hours sleep or I'd pass out on the chair I was occupying.

"Okay."

"That's it? Just okay?"

"If it will be easier for you to accept the fact I'm not human while giving me your trust so I can protect you, I will be a vampire." A soft breeze gently grazed the skin on my neck exposed from the ponytail, coming from behind me. I fought the need to smile. "I'll even be a shifter if it'll help you process better. Just don't ask me to purr while you scratch my belly, and I'm not good at hacking out hairballs."

The owlish look on her face was priceless.

"You're getting better at noticing my presence." Dominic's rasp as he entered the small room sent a shiver down my back. "I was being stealthier than usual."

I didn't point out that after our conversation, when he shared why he wanted revenge, I'd been too aware of him for my own well-being. His scent reached me just a moment before I felt the shift in the air. My every nerve ending was honed to him like a tuning fork. No matter what I was doing, including running for my life with Johnathan slung over my shoulder, I knew every move he made, every twitch of a muscle. If I was smart, I would've been worried. Considering I was on the run from the deadliest masters of the underground, how smart I actually was might be debatable.

" I can learn a few new tricks …" I kept my tone conversational as he stepped out from behind me, aiming for the third and only other armchair in the room. "… occasionally."

"Mhhh …" The rumble came from deep in his chest as he lowered himself, a heavy sigh falling from his lips. Goose-bumps appeared on my arms when I took in his muscular form and tousled hair.

"Well?" Alice was frowning at the shifter. "Are you going to tell us, or do I have to pull the words out of your mouth every time. What is wrong with you guys? We all know what's happening, so telling without waiting to be asked is what normal people do."

"For one, we are not people, human." There was no fire in Dominic's tone, but it made Alice cringe anyway. My hand clenched in a fist seeing her reaction, but I didn't think punching the shifter would solve any problems. We were all tired and snappy. "As for the scum, he hasn't woken yet."

The intensity of his green eyes when they landed on my face took my breath away. It was almost a physical sensation, as if he reached inside me to grab hold of my lungs and squeezed. His animal stared at me through his irises with a primal, predatory glint, as if he was challenging me. Daring me to even twitch so I would become his hunted prey. Something that should've fired up my instincts and made me lunge for his throat, but it didn't.

"That is unusual. It was only a broken neck." Realizing my hand had moved to reach for my pendant, I lowered it immediately.

It didn't go unnoticed by Dominic, but he was kind enough not to say anything about it. Veronica's voice floated through my mind *"You're slipping. Pay attention."* And with it, a fist squeezed around my lungs and cut off all the oxygen from passing my airways.

"Which would make any normal person meet his maker," Alice muttered under her breath, but I ignored the comment. My human friend, although very open-minded, still struggled with the concept of creatures like us existing outside of fiction books.

"I wouldn't insult you by asking if you are sure, and he

is not pretending," I told Dominic as an offhanded compliment, which earned me a twitch of his mouth.

"Is there a way he could prolong the healing knowing there is an interrogation waiting for him the moment he is awake?" Although his tone was even, I couldn't help noticing the dark smudges under the shifter's eyes. He's been at it day and night ever since we got here.

Me? I've tried my best to pretend we didn't have an unconscious male tied to a chair in the basement. My past and my present threatened to crash on top of my head, and I was determined to ignore it until the bitter end.

"We can control our healing, to a point." Searching his gaze, I debated how much to tell him. Airing out our weaknesses would do me no good if he decided he didn't want to play nice anymore and start his revenge on the Syndicate with me. Nothing in his behavior so far said he would do that, but better be safe than sorry. "I think we should all get some rest first. I'm too tired to deal with the likes of him, and I might end up killing the one person that could give us the answers we need. I will check on Johnathan after I wake up. Now we sleep. Including you, Alice."

"I don't feel like sleeping. I'm not tired," was her immediate rebuke a second before a big yawn made her jaw crack. Like a young child, my friend was afraid she would miss something if she didn't keep an eye on us at all times.

"You were saying, human?" Dominic glowered at her.

"I'm not a toddler, and you are not my father, cat," Alice snarked, folding her arms across her chest stubbornly. If I wasn't forcing my eyes to stay open, I would've laughed at the expression on Dominic's face. "You can't send me to bed."

"But I can." I should've thought better of it before kneeling in front of her chair and locking her in my gaze.

"Sleep." Alice slumped in the recliner, her features softening immediately as her breathing evened out.

I froze, my heart lodging in my throat.

Swallowing thickly, my head turned slowly to the side, and my gaze locked on Dominic's. The shifter was as tense as I was, while his green irises burned all the way to my core. I could see the emotions playing on his features when he realized I had the power of mind control. It all played out from shock, to rage and finally settled on suspicion. What little headway I made with him to build trust between us shattered like a house made of glass under a giant's foot. Tears prickled the back of my eyes as I called myself stupid many times in my head. Knowing that Alice would force herself to stay awake, I didn't think about what I was doing. All I wanted was for my human friend to get some rest, and by idiotically acting on impulse, I showed Dominic something that not even Veronica knew.

Panic clawed my insides.

A muscle ticked in Dominic's jaw before his lips parted. I braced myself for whatever accusations he was about to throw at me, but he thought better of it. Clamping his lips shut in a firm line, he shook his head and uncurled from the armchair, fists clenched at his sides. Since I was still kneeling in front of Alice, I had to crane my neck to keep eye contact with him. A flutter in my chest told me I expected him to attack. My entire body was poised in preparation for it. He stood looming over me for a few long moments before turning on his heel and stomping out of the small room.

"Take the human to her bed. She will be useless if we need to run tomorrow if she sleeps in that chair." He snarled over his shoulder before closing the door.

I released the breath I was holding after he was gone. Just because he walked away didn't mean he wouldn't attack. Clenching my jaw, I lifted Alice in my arms. There would be no sleeping for me this day.

At last, I'd be alert if we were discovered during the daytime. There was a silver lining in everything.

Grab your copy…
vinci-books.com/lowerworld

About the Author

Maya Daniels, USA Today Bestselling and multi-award-winning supernatural suspense author, is a fun-loving woman with many talents.

She traveled the world, gaining life experiences that helped her career as an investigative journalist, as well as her storytelling. Maya writes compelling tales of magic, mythical creatures, loyalty, and life-changing friendships with snarky female characters—much like herself.

Her travels have taken her to Europe, Africa, Asia, Australia, and America. Born with her feet in motion, she currently resides in Ohio, spinning her next epic story that you will not want to put down.

Her biggest 'sins' are her love of chocolate and coffee—through an IV drip! One to never sit still, Maya practices Reiki healing, different types of martial arts, reads about the arcane, talks to furry creatures more than humans, picks up a sledgehammer for home improvement, and travels with her fated mate, seeking her own adventures.

www.ingramcontent.com/pod-product-compliance
Lightning Source LLC
Chambersburg PA
CBHW011749010726
47498CB00012B/2987